THE MAN WHO WALKED ON WATER

JACOB BEAVER

This is a work of fiction. Names, characters, places, and incidents are products of the author's imagination or are used fictitiously and are not to be construed as real. Any resemblance to actual events, locales, organizations, or persons, living or dead, is entirely coincidental.

HarperCollins books may be purchased for educational, business, or sales promotional use. For information, please email the Special Markets Department at SPsales@harpercollins.com.

ISBN 978-0-06-267463-0

To my mother and sister, back at home,
and to my wife, Linda,
here at home

Part 1

You have probably heard of my brother, Stephen Mallory, the daredevil English reporter who parachutes into war zones armed only with a video camera. He is famous now, which is what he always wanted. One day Hollywood will make a movie about him. That's where he lives—Hollywood, or somewhere nearby. I've never been to his house, although I live in America too. But I live in a different America, far away in the mountains of North Carolina. I'm happy here. I feel blessed every day, and for that I thank God. Also, strangely, I thank Stephen. So, Steve, if you ever read this, please try to regard it as a kind of long thank-you note. You will hate me for it, no doubt, but I am not out to slander you or settle old scores. My aim is to tell the truth about certain events that changed the course of my life. As it says in Galatians, "Am I therefore become your enemy, because I tell you the truth?"

Ten years ago, when nobody had heard of Stephen Mallory, when he was just another freelance journalist running around London, he made a short film called *The Man Who Walked on Water*. You can google it if you like. I haven't bothered to google it because I was there during the filming—because I am still there, in a sense. And anyway, it's an awful film. My brother is an idiot. I love him because he's my younger brother, but Steve always was loud and crass, stupid about people and the mysteries of other lives. What Steve likes is Big Ideas. Ten years ago, Steve's Big Idea was to fly out to East Tennessee, where a man had reportedly walked on water, and to get this man on film, suspended between heaven and earth, water lapping his toes. Or to expose the man as a fraud. Or both. Whatever happened, the title of the film would sell it, he hoped. The BBC hoped so too. They gave Steve £20,000.

At the time, I was living back at home with our parents. Aged thirty-five, I was in my old bedroom again, at the top of the house, gazing across Muswell Hill at the evening lights of North London, just as I'd done as a teenager. The difference now was that those twinkling lights didn't beckon me. They held no radiant promise. I had planned to be a rock star, and the plan had failed. So I fell into other things, as failed rockers do—as most of us do. I became a "set technician" for TV ads, or in other words, a carpenter. And I met a girl, and we bought a nice flat, and I was happy for a number of years. Looking back, I *was* happy. *She* wasn't, evidently. One day she told me she'd met someone, and a week later she was gone. This someone turned out to be a hotshot TV producer, a rising star. I knew the guy. I'd worked for him once. I'd liked him. Now I hated him, of course, and I hated myself. I hated the whole world, all those lovely twinkling lights. Their loveliness made me cry, standing there in my old bedroom, late at night and drunk, very drunk.

I realize now that I was having a breakdown, a collapse, a falling apart. I don't know what to call it, precisely, but I do know that I had been heading there for a long time, perhaps my whole life. Back then, I understood nothing. All I knew was that life was hell. When I think of those days, what I remember most is a kind of blackness around the edge of things. It's hard to explain, but the blackness seemed to creep over me, like the blackness that engulfs the screen at the end of those old Looney Tunes cartoons, shrinking the circle of light down and down until . . . *That's all Folks!* Sometimes, as I rode my motorbike to work, weaving through the London traffic, the darkness would descend and I almost closed my eyes. How simple it would be. Just twist the accelerator and . . . That's all, folks.

Also, I was drinking. I drank in pubs at lunchtime, in restaurants after work, at home alone. Often I'd end up half naked in front of my laptop, surrounded by empty wine bottles and ogling beautiful women as they caressed themselves to ecstasy. In the morning I'd have a hangover and another bill on my credit card. The mornings were terrible.

One such morning, a Saturday, Steve showed up. I was lying facedown on the sofa in the living room. My mother was washing up breakfast and my father was raking leaves in the back garden. They were in their sixties. My father had just retired from the police force, and he was happy about it. He could easily spend the whole day doing small jobs that no one else cared about, like raking leaves and stuffing them into green plastic bags. Stupid, I thought. I think differently now. My father cared about the little details of his life, of our lives, which is another way of saying that he loved us. Since he died, three years ago, the garden has gone wild.

I was half asleep when Steve walked into the living room and started yelling at me. Steve always yells. He was born with the volume turned way up. Because everything excites him. That day he was excited to eat breakfast—my mother had made him poached eggs, his favorite—and he was excited about a new pair of shoes he'd bought, with springs in the heels, which made you bounce as you walked. I heard Steve telling my mother about this in the kitchen, and then he bounced back into the living room and slapped me on the head.

"Wake up, fuckface!" he said. "I want to talk to you."

I sat up, very slowly, feeling that darkness at the edge of things.

Steve was wearing a tight blue suit with a silvery sheen. I had to smile. I'd never seen Steve in anything but jeans and T-shirts. Baggy T-shirts. Steve is short and chubby, with thin blond hair that sort of floats around the top of his head. With his pale eyes and his silver-blue suit bulging at the shoulders and thighs, he looked like the mad killer in a gangster movie. And the bouncy shoes didn't help. They had thick black soles and seemed orthopedic—an outward symbol of the killer's crippled insides.

"What?" he said.

"That," I said, pointing.

"This? This is classy. Cost me three hundred quid. I'm trying to look serious here. I've got stuff *going on*. I can't lie around on sofas all day. And neither can you."

"Oh, piss off."

Steve just nodded, as if time would tell—and it did, actually. But I was annoyed. Steve is seven years younger than me, yet he always bosses me around. He bosses everyone except my mother. And somehow, amazingly, he gets away with it. People do what he says. He has no charm at all, quite the opposite. What he has is energy. Energy flares off him, like the silvery light on his ridiculous suit. And it sparks other people. It wakes you up. It woke *me* up that Saturday morning, because I could see that something was coming. And here it was:

"Now listen, I've got a proposition," Steve said. He hunched down on our father's footstool, stretching the seams of his suit. "John-Boy, this is good for you and me. There's money here. Travel, too."

My name is John. John-Boy was an old family joke. When Steve called me John-Boy, I knew I was in trouble. Steve can be relentless when he wants something from you. My father and I called him the Terminator, another old family joke.

So, Steve told me about his Big Idea and the BBC money, and I congratulated him. It *was* impressive. Even Steve seemed impressed with himself. He said, "I'm still in shock. Twenty grand! And I'm a nobody!"

"Well, you've got a degree in journalism. You've had stuff in the Sunday papers."

Steve scowled. "The BBC don't give a shit about that. I'm a chancer, and they know it. But I do have something." He paused and spread his hands, like a magician revealing a rabbit. "I have Florentino Pagazzi."

Now I laughed, despite my hangover, despite the blackness looming around us. Even on my worst days, I still had a sense of humor. Something could make me laugh when I was dying inside, which didn't make sense to me until recently, when I realized that laughter isn't about happiness. Laughter is a ripple of light from above, a parting of the dark seas, a glimpse of forever. Make of that what you will. I believe it deeply, but I can't explain myself.

Anyway, Steve told me that Florentino Pagazzi was an award-winning cameraman, a friend of his, who knew people at the BBC.

"It's all about who you know, right?" Steve said.

Wrong, wrong. I disagreed completely. Who you know is irrelevant. Lots of people knew Saddam Hussein, and look where that got them. Saddam Hussein was now on the run, and Iraq was in ruins. Right then I could hear gunfire from the kitchen, where my mother was watching TV. (A few years later and Steve would be on that TV, running towards the gunfire.) No, the point is whether you *like* the people you know. Do you admire them? Do they inspire you? But I said nothing. Steve wouldn't have listened anyhow. He was busy telling me that £20,000 really wasn't that much, once you'd factored in the fees for Florentino and his soundman, plus flights and hotels, plus editing costs, and on and on. What it came down to was that Steve needed an assistant, and he'd picked me for the job, and that's why he was pacing around our parents' living room in his shiny blue suit, waving his arms and glancing at his watch. He had a business lunch in an hour, he said, and then he was going to book the flights. I had to make up my mind now, this moment. Yes or no?

I said yes. Why I said it I still don't know. I could have resisted the Terminator. I could have told him I had lots of work on, which wasn't true but who cares? I could have told him I didn't feel like getting on a plane with people I'd never met, and flying to a foreign country for reasons that were unclear at best, and that would lead to nothing for me except discomfort and lack of sleep. I could have said I didn't even want to get off the sofa. But I didn't. I said yes, and for that, and for what happened after that, I thank Steve.

———

Three days later we all met at Heathrow. The airport was crowded. I remember that because I arrived first, and I stood near the check-in desks trying to spot Steve among the elderly autumn holidaymakers. Many of them wore hiking shoes and hi-tech, multipocketed costumes. English people are weird like that. When they leave the country, they buy all these clothes they'd never normally wear, as if travel requires a kind of military preparedness. Most of them were probably going to Greece or southern Spain, but they looked like they were headed for outer space.

I was wearing what I always wore—boots, jeans, leather jacket—and hoping it wasn't too hot in Tennessee. I have to admit I didn't know where Tennessee was. I only knew it was in the South, which made me think of *Forrest Gump* and *Gone with the Wind* and *Deliverance*. If we'd been going to New York I'd have thought of *Goodfellas*. My ideas about America all came from movies. In fact, most of my ideas about the world came from film and TV, much of it American. I'd never been anywhere outside Britain, apart from a couple of holidays in Mediterranean resorts full of Brits, which didn't really count. So, although I wasn't dressed like the people around me, I understood how they felt. For me, Tennessee *was* outer space.

I spotted Steve's fair hair floating through the crowd, and I waved to him. He grimaced back at me. Steve could hardly walk, let alone wave. He had a backpack slung over one shoulder, a laptop over the other, and a briefcase in each hand. He dropped all this stuff around him and stood there panting. I just stood there. I mean, I didn't say anything, because I didn't have anything to say. We're brothers. We don't make polite conversation. Of course, I had lots of questions about Tennessee, but Steve couldn't answer them. He had only been to America once, the year before. He'd flown to Miami, with a photographer, to do an article about bums living among the super-rich. Steve had strolled along the beach handing out cash in exchange for photographs and life stories. The photos were so sad. You can imagine them: dirty people drinking from paper bags as night falls over glittering seafront condos. Steve called his article "The End of the American Dream." That was his Big Idea at the time. But what did Steve know about American dreams? More to the point, what did he know about Tennessee? I had asked him this. He'd told me we were going to *East* Tennessee, which was mountains. Then he said something about hillbillies and banjos. In other words, *Deliverance*. Like me, he was thinking of movies.

Florentino Pagazzi was another story. He'd been everywhere, it seemed. As soon as he appeared, I understood why Steve liked him.

Tino, as he called himself, was in his early fifties. He was small and wiry and tanned golden brown. All of him was golden brown, including the dome of his head, which was smooth and spotted, like a speckled egg. The most striking thing about him, though, was his eyes. They never stopped moving. As he approached us, wheeling several cases and bags, and even as he shook hands with me, his dark eyes flickered about, scanning the crowd, as if something might happen at any moment. What he was hoping to see, I don't know, but he was always like this, *looking*. And he always had a faint smile. The smile told you that he was friendly, up to a point, and that he was a man of the world. Both things were true.

As we waited for the soundman, I learned that Tino had shot films on every continent. Back in the 1970s he'd filmed a documentary about the Appalachian Trail, for French TV, and he joked about his troubles with the Tennessee accent. His own accent was pure Italian, all teeth and tongue. Although he was based in London and spoke a rattling, exuberant English, he never said hello or goodbye. It was always "Ciao!"

"Ciao!" he said now, eyes darting, as a man walked towards us carrying a large metal case. The man set his case down slowly. Then he straightened slowly. Then he took a slow, deep breath and said, "Hey."

The man's name was Dave something—Smith maybe, or Brown. I've forgotten now. Everything about him was instantly forgettable. During the whole trip I don't think he spoke more than fifty full sentences. All I remember is his BO, which stayed in my nose, and the round birthmark on the back of his neck, exactly like a button you might push. I doubt anyone had ever pushed it. Dave was about my age, unmarried, probably permanently, and nothing seemed to surprise him, to rouse him, to buck him up, not even my brother. He wasn't melancholy. He just seemed to have a very, very slow pulse. Perhaps that's why he was a good sound-man. When the chips were down and the moment was upon you, the fleeting moment at which the camera was pointed, any small mistake spelled disaster. At least that was how Tino behaved. Dave simply held up the microphone and eyed his equipment.

We got our boarding passes and queued at passport control, and then Steve and Tino charged off through duty-free. Despite his size, Tino moved fast, and Steve bounced right along with him in his bouncy shoes, leaving me and Dave yards behind—which set the pattern for the trip. That was fine with me. I was happy to follow behind with Dave, since Dave required zero conversation and I could think my own thoughts. Right then I was looking out at the jumbo jets on the tarmac and wondering at the immense power that kept them in the air. I had only flown twice in my life, on smaller planes. They creaked and lurched about, as if they might come apart, and I threw up both times. This looked worse. Jumbo jets were *heavy*. What would happen if an engine failed? Was there a backup? Or could the plane fly with one engine? Wouldn't it go in circles, spiraling down and down and down, until . . . That's all, folks.

I had an aisle seat on the plane, in the middle row, next to a skinny woman with red hair. I still think about that woman sometimes. Her face was like a knuckle, white and bony. Beside her were two boys—a little kid and a toddler. They had the same red hair and knuckle faces, and both wore black skullcaps. As the plane taxied for takeoff, all three bowed their heads and started murmuring. Then we rocketed into the sky. The plane climbed sickeningly and banked hard. Spread out below me, intricate as a circuit board and seemingly endless, was West London. My heart skipped a beat, it really did. But here's the thing: no one else even glanced out the window. On my left, the mother and her two sons were still mumbling into their laps. On my right, across the aisle, Steve was tapping at his big silver PowerBook. Beside him, a woman was thumbing the in-flight magazine, and behind them a young couple were screwing in their earbuds. Really? I thought. You don't care? In the blink of an eye you're thousands of feet up in the air, and the view down doesn't *interest* you? I suppose they'd all seen such views on TV, in higher definition. So why bother with it? Change the channel. In fact, most people around me were doing just that—changing the channels on their seat-back video screens, looking for something good. But what does "good" mean? There's a question. It's the kind of question I ask myself a lot these days, now that I am beginning to know who I am, and to understand the hell I carry inside myself.

Again I say, make of that what you will. I'm talking with hindsight. As I sat on that plane, I was merely surprised by the behavior of the other passengers. The man in front of me was the most surprising. He'd been jabbing the controls of his video screen, and now he barked at a passing stewardess.

"This blimming thing won't work," the man said. "What am I meant to do for eight hours? Don't tell me I'm in economy and so I just have to sit here and twiddle my thumbs. Sod that. I want an upgrade."

The stewardess made soothing noises and fingered the controls, but the man kept barking. I thought he might hit someone. It was entirely possible he'd make a break for business class and go down fighting. He was a tough character. From what I could see of him, he looked about sixty, but his neck bulged with muscle and his hair was jet black. Thankfully, his screen came on and the stewardess sashayed off. But the man wasn't done yet. He pushed his seat back into my knees, then gave another mighty push, which achieved nothing although it hurt me. I winced, and the woman beside me smiled. Her kids were watching cartoons. She sat with her hands folded.

"Excuse me," I said. "Do you mind if I ask you something? What were you doing just now, as we took off?"

"I was praying to God," she said. "We are in God's hands."

Then she closed her eyes.

I sat back and watched someone's video screen across the aisle. The screen showed a map of Europe, with a red line tracing our path over Northern Ireland and out to sea. Altitude was 36,000 feet and ground speed 600 mph. Wow! We were hurtling through the stratosphere. I'd never have guessed it. Now that the plane had leveled out, the ride was smooth as could be. The only movement was a slight vibration under my feet, which I liked. I slipped off my shoes and looked right, past Steve's profile, at a fairyland of cloud mountains and cloud castles, all pearly white against the infinite blue—and suddenly I felt okay. I felt almost hopeful. It was like I'd been loosed from my own life, from the creeping darkness that sucked light and air, and suddenly I could see, I could breathe. My lungs filled with the cool stream blowing from the vent above me, and I stretched out my legs so that my heels shook softy and sent soft shakes further upwards . . .

It was then that Steve explained the job to me. He leaned across the aisle and started yelling at low volume, which is his version of whispering. Normally I'd have pretended to listen, and made ironic comments to maintain the pretense, but Steve picked the perfect moment. At that precise point in that day, in that month, that year, floating in midair and in midlife, balanced between despair and hope, darkness and light, I was ready to hear what Steve had to tell me. "I'm all ears," our father used to say. That was me, turning to Steve—all ears.

My job was to get clearances, Steve said. Anyone who appeared in the film had to sign something called a *model release*, which avoided any chance of litigation against Steve or the BBC. It was just a page of small print. There was also a longer document called a *life rights consent agreement*, which the subject of the film had to sign because we were telling his life story, but Steve would handle that, once everything else was agreed.

"What have you agreed so far?" I asked.

"Nothing."

"Well, what's this guy expecting?"

"He's not expecting anything," Steve said. "I haven't contacted him."

"You're joking!"

"Look, the man doesn't have a phone. Doesn't have email. Doesn't have a *computer*. He's off the grid, you know. What could I do?"

"You could send a letter."

Steve sighed. "A letter, right. I didn't think of that. Anyhow it doesn't matter. The bloke will be there. That's his thing, being available to all and sundry. He's some kind of preacher, a very holy-type person, all about saving your soul."

"So you've researched this in depth?" I said. I couldn't help it. But Steve missed the sarcasm.

"Yeah, I've dug around," he said. "Didn't find anything, actually. That's how you know you're onto a winner. This is virgin territory."

"So how do you even know about . . . what's this man called?"

"Buckner," Steve said. "Lee Buckner. There was a tiny piece about him in the *Metro*. Just a few lines, no photo. Man walks on water in East Tennessee, basically. It was a summary of a syndicated article, which wasn't very big in the first place, and hardly any papers picked it up. The woman who wrote it is a journalist in Johnson City. I phoned her and got what she had, which isn't much. Only one person would go on record, this old man. He said he was fishing on a lake early one morning and Buckner walked out of the mist, right in front of his boat. Spooky, huh? Other people have seen him too, apparently. We've got to find those people and get them to sign the clearance forms. Then we interview the fuck out of them. And that's the plan. That's it. Apart from filming Buckner walk on water, of course."

Steve grinned.

I said, "So what's the point? He isn't going to walk on water, obviously. It won't happen."

"I don't know," Steve said. "And you don't know either. We think we know, but we don't. It's called belief, and *that* is the point. It's all a question of what you believe. A religious person might believe something different. Right?"

"What does it matter?" I said. "He still can't walk on water."

"Oh, he can," Steve said. "He does it somehow, and I'm going to see him do it. I got twenty grand on the line here. It'll happen, don't you worry. I know what I'm doing."

"You *think* you know," I said. "You believe."

Steve looked at me. "Okay, I believe."

And he went back to his laptop.

I thought no more about our conversation, not at the time anyway. The film was Steve's baby. As it happened, though, my mind turned to religion again. After we ate, my neighbor produced a fat book, like a Bible, and began clucking to her kids. It sounded like clucking, I mean. I guessed it was Hebrew. Then they all bowed their heads again, but this time in silence. I pretended not to look, though I wasn't sure why. Partly it was that praying seemed very personal, like crying, but mostly I just didn't know what to do. I'd never been around people who prayed. There had been a few Pakistani Muslims at my secondary school, and one Sikh boy, and other kids used to tease them about their religions, but I never saw them *do* anything religious. And our family didn't go to church. Nobody's family went to church. I honestly don't think I knew what churches were for. Even when my girlfriend ran off with the TV producer, and I was marooned in a half-empty flat, all alone, all at once, like a shipwreck survivor gazing at broken pieces of his ship, even then it didn't occur to me to pray. I just sat in the living room and stared at a space on the wall where a picture used to be. I sat there all day, until it got dark, and then I went out to the pub and got so drunk I forgot she'd left me.

The only other thing I remember about that flight happened right at the end, in Atlanta, as we were waiting to leave the plane. The Jewish toddler had been fidgeting for an hour or so. His mother tried to control him, but he kept pushing her away, and finally she slapped him on the wrist. He screamed. Man, did he scream. His little white knuckle face went red, and his mouth stretched wide, and he screamed and screamed. People were bunched in the aisles, yawning and gathering their stuff and making phone calls, and this kid went on screaming, and screaming, and screaming.

The man in front of me, the tough guy, stood up and turned around. His face was fleshy and pockmarked, and there was something funny about his eyes, like they weren't moving in sync. He looked down at the screaming toddler. Then he raised a hand to his head, made a fist, and removed his jet-black hair.

He was bald.

The toddler went quiet. Other people went quiet too. The man didn't seem to notice. He made no expression at all, simply replaced his wig and turned back around.

I'll never forget that moment. It was wonderful. That's a strange thing to say, I know, but it was a strange moment, strange and full of wonder.

———

The airport in Atlanta is big. It's the main hub for the South, full of people changing planes. Since that first trip I've been there many times, in different seasons and at different hours, and it's always the same, cool and hushed, TVs playing low, announcements off in the distance. Everyone plods down these long corridors, looking a bit dreamy, as if travel were a kind of sleepwalking between time zones. I go dreamy too, these days. The first time, though, when I stepped off the plane and walked down the Jetway passage, I was crackling with adrenaline.

America!

I saw two soldiers in camouflage, with buzz cuts and tall boots. I thought they were guarding the airport, but they didn't have guns. Then I noticed their bags. And then I saw an old black man talking to someone, and as I walked past he said, "Shee-it!" He said it with delight, grinning and shaking his head, like in a movie. And then I saw a pretty girl in capri pants, like a movie, and two young boys in sunglasses, like a movie, and a large woman in a turtleneck, with jewelry hanging *over* the turtleneck, like a movie . . .

And then I crashed. At least I don't remember much else, apart from sitting at a departure gate for hours, wishing I could lie down. Eventually we trooped outside into a warm wind and filed across a stretch of tarmac. In front of us was a small plane with its taillight winking in the dusk. Within minutes we were off. We roared through darkness, peering down at clusters of lights, and then at nothing at all, and suddenly we dropped out of the darkness and there were yellow streetlights just below us, and a few cars, and next thing we were on the ground, roaring to a stop.

By now I was woozy with tiredness and nothing made sense. Why was it cold here? Why was the airport so empty? What did the rental car guy mean by "your John Hancock"? Which of these identical, shiny red SUVs was ours? And most puzzling of all, where was Johnson City? We were driving through it, with Steve at the wheel and Tino reading the map, but I couldn't *see* it. All I saw was grassy fields, some houses and churches, a couple of supermarkets, and then a long row of lighted signs, mostly fast food. One of the signs said ABC INN—*Sleep Cheap!*—which was where we stayed that night. Steve and I shared a room. Neither of us said a word, just hit the sack.

I woke at dawn. The place was silent. Not a sound inside or out, except for the hum of a fan heater below the window. I watched the curtains billow and bloom with light. Then I dressed quietly and went out.

The door opened onto a car park—or parking lot, I should say. There was our shiny red SUV. Beyond it lay a strip of grass and then another parking lot, this one enormous and ending with a line of glassy shopfronts—or storefronts, I should say. Around the parking lot were trees, the most beautiful trees. They hadn't been planted there. These were big trees, old trees, and they glowed with color. Leaves tumbled in the wind like confetti, red and orange and yellow. Against the falling leaves, the sky was solid blue, all the way to the horizon, which was dark and wavy and looked like mountains.

That's East Tennessee. That's North Carolina, too. In a sense, that's all of America—a world of beauty shimmering behind strip malls. But I didn't know this. I only knew what I saw: the cracked gray asphalt dotted with cigarette butts, and then these bright falling leaves. Like a baby, I was stuck in the moment, without history. How could I tell where I was? I had no points of reference apart from movies, and movies are dreams. They flash and fade.

Now a dented pickup rolled into the parking lot. It stopped ten yards away and a man got out, a bearded man in brown overalls. He took a toolbox from the back of the truck and came towards me, across the strip of grass, into the motel parking lot.

"Sure is purdy, ain't it?" he said.

I said, "Sorry?"

"The leaves," he said. "Jest so purdy. If they was any purdier I couldn't stand it."

He smiled, and I smiled too, and then he walked on towards the motel lobby.

I bent down and picked up a small leaf and tucked it into my shirt pocket. I still have that leaf. It's from a maple of some kind, maybe an Autumn Blaze, and it is red as blood. At first I kept it flattened in a wad of clearance forms, but later I put it in my Bible. It marks 2 Corinthians 5:17, one of my favorite passages:

"Therefore if any man be in Christ, he is a new creature: old things are passed away; behold, all things are become new."

———

We ate breakfast at a diner, which took some time because the meals were huge, and also because the waitress wouldn't leave us alone. She was old, this waitress, with a sad gray face, but she shivered with joy when Steve ordered steak and eggs. "I used to know a man from England," she said. "He spoke like you, real proper. Everything he said, I mean every little thing, oh, it sounded so sweet. I wanted to marry him just to hear him talk! Say something else, honey. How you like your eggs?"

That became a running joke between me and Tino. Whenever Steve was ordering me about or yelling too much, I'd tell him to say something else, honey, I just love to hear you talk. Steve didn't care. Mockery doesn't touch Steve. Even when he was small and I teased him, he would never cry.

Anyway, we left the diner and drove out of Johnson City, and now I understood why I couldn't see it the night before. Johnson City wasn't so much a place as *pieces* of a place. What I mean is, the buildings were all grouped in separate developments: a mall here, a subdivision there, some car showrooms, office buildings, a Wal-mart . . . Between these scattered pieces were rolling hills of green, topped with bursts of fall color, all of it crystal clear beneath the blue, blue sky. The roads were wide and empty—or rather, they seemed empty to me. The traffic was mostly pickup trucks and big cars, some of them shooting past and others grinding along in terrible shape, as if they'd rolled off a cliff or something. Soon the road narrowed and began to curve upwards, past clapboard houses and barns of weathered wood, a trailer park, a little white church with a sign saying GOD ANSWERS KNEE-MAIL, then fields with cows, and more fields with cows, and suddenly—

Mountains.

We crested a rise and there they were, not ten miles away, one after another after another, like a sea of vast frozen waves fading to blue.

"Holy shit," Steve said, pulling off the road. "Hey Tino, how's that for an establishing shot? This is where the film starts, right here. Look at it! It's got everything. Mystery, isolation. The power of the primitive. This is bloody *brilliant*."

So Tino set up his camera, and Dave recorded some birdsong, and then we drove on down through woods of amber and ruby, with great branches overhanging the road like colored chandeliers. We came out beside a lake. It was maybe a mile across, with ruffled blue water. There were a few houses along the shore, then a marina with floating boat docks, and then we were back in the woods, zigzagging upwards. I opened my window. The air

smelled great. It smelled of earth and rain. I let it flow into me
as we climbed past some ruined houses, a trailer covered in ivy,
a gas station with three old men on a bench, laughing in the
sunshine . . .

Again I had that glorious feeling, as if I'd been loosed from my
own life, as if I'd been somehow lifted out of it, into a realm of
light and loveliness, into this airy moment.

Now we dropped through the trees and saw the lake again,
much wider here, with two buildings by the shore. The first building was timbered, with a red roof, and looked to me like a ski
lodge. The sign said SHELBY'S BAR & BARBECUE. The second building, of pale brick, was wide and low, with an empty swimming
pool at the side. The sign said SHELBY MOTEL.

Steve pulled into the parking lot of the motel, next to the only
other car. He bounced off in his silly shoes, and I borrowed the map
from Tino. I didn't learn much, because the map didn't show much,
just a couple of wiggly roads and the wiggly blue fingers of the lake,
which was called Watauga Lake. A patch of green surrounded the
blue: Cherokee National Forest. Cherokee? I knew that name. Wer-
en't they the Indians in some dusty western? But how could that be,
here in the southeast among these wooded mountains?

"I booked us a room each," Steve said, opening the back of
the SUV. "Apparently this is the only hotel for miles. We're close,
though. Buckner lives up the road somewhere. Let's unload our
bags and then go see."

The Shelby Motel was classic Americana. Standing outside,
looking at the row of numbered doors, I was reminded of a thousand movies, from *Psycho* to *Pulp Fiction*. In fact I was more than
reminded, a lot more. For a second or two, I had the eerie sensa-
tion that I was *in* a movie, some kind of ultrarealistic 3D movie
with warm sunlight and a cool breeze. Even nowadays, after ten
years in America, the same thing happens. I'll be driving somewhere and I'll see a white picket fence, and all of a sudden I'm in

Technicolor. Maybe manic depressives feel this way when they're up, as if the world just exploded in their face. Of course, manic depressives are delusional, and so is this feeling. The world is what it is, if only we could see it. Ten years ago, standing in that parking lot, all I could see was myself—but that was about to change. It started changing a moment later, when I walked into the office of the Shelby Motel and a young woman smiled at me.

She had the greenest eyes. They were green like a cat's eyes are green, piercing green, and they shot green holes in me. I could hardly take in the rest of her or smile back. Then Steve came in behind me, asking about keys, and I saw that the woman had one arm. The left sleeve of her blouse was pinned to her waist.

"I've given you rooms four to seven," she said. "Take your pick. They're all the same."

Her voice was soft and slightly husky, with a certain lilt to it. I assumed that lilt was southern, which it was, but at the same time it was entirely her own. We all talk differently, don't we? Anyhow, I liked her voice. To be honest, I loved her voice. It seemed to fall over me like a gentle rain.

Steve said, "Tell me again. Where does Lee Buckner live?"

The green eyes widened, perhaps in amusement. "Oh, I don't know where he lives. I said I know where his church is. He uses a big old barn."

I didn't hear the rest of their conversation. I was just watching the woman. Her hair was dark and long, cut just above those green eyes. Her skin was tanned, very tanned, with a dusting of freckles. Against the tan, her teeth seemed incredibly white.

Now a phone rang.

The woman said, "The road ain't got a sign, but you'll see it. It's just around the curve, on the right." And she picked up the phone.

As Steve and I walked back outside, I heard the woman say, "You've reached the Shelby Motel. I'm Summer. How may I help you?"

———

"Just around the curve" is like "up yonder" and "down the road a piece." It's the southern way of being friendly, which means putting you at ease, making you feel happy about your day. It's nothing to do with distance. In fact, "the curve" went on for a good mile, and the road to the right snaked into deep woods. This road was narrow and freshly paved but without markings. It might have been a private driveway if not for the odd mailbox by a gravel track. I didn't see a single house, or a car, or a person. I didn't see any animals. I saw tree trunks and leaves and shafts of yellow sunlight filled with falling leaves, and leaves mashed into the asphalt ahead of us, like gold flecks in black granite.

Then I saw the blue of water. The lake appeared on our left, below us, with a dead tree lying a little way out. The opposite bank wasn't far, not more than a stone's throw. A boy stood at the edge, among the trees, holding a fishing pole. He was pulling back on the fishing pole and I was trying to see if he'd got a fish, when Tino sang out.

"*Alt! Alt!*" he said. "Stop, Steve!"

Steve stopped.

On the hillside above us was a huge sign, the size of a billboard. It was made of bare plywood and was badly weathered, but the words were clear enough. They had been painted in black, very boldly, and looked something like this:

CHURCH OF GOD

ALWAYS OPEN

SIMPLE AS THAT!

Steve edged off the road at the bottom of a steep driveway, and Tino jumped out of the car. By the time I got out, he was nearly up the driveway. Beyond him, on top of the hill, stood a massive barn.

It was taller than the tallest houses around here, with a sharply pitched roof, not unlike a church. But it was in bad shape. One corner was collapsing, and the whole roof was red with rust. Even back then, when I knew nothing about tobacco barns, I could tell this building was ancient. It was clad with vertical planks, hundreds of them, and they'd turned the color of driftwood. The total effect was beautiful, a sort of dancing silvery gray. One thing spoiled it, though. In the center of the barn, framed by a section of new timber, was a white door. It was the kind of door you see on suburban homes, with fake leaded glass. It looked like my parents' door, actually.

Tino knocked on the door. He put his face to the glass, then knocked again. Then he opened the door and disappeared.

I crossed the road and looked down at an old house half hidden by trees. Three pickup trucks sat beside the house on a patch of red dirt. Only one of them had wheels. Beyond the pickups was a concrete ramp that went into the lake. I couldn't see a boat, and the top of the ramp was covered in weeds. The driveway to the house was weedy too. There were even some weeds on top of the house.

As I turned back, Tino came skipping down the hill. He stopped halfway and looked around, and then he looked at us and gave a big shrug. Right at that moment, there was a gunshot. I mean, it sounded like I imagined a gunshot would sound. I'd never heard a gun go off. I'd never been near a gun, except in video games.

At that time, Steve hadn't been around guns either, as far as I know. Perhaps this was the moment when he discovered his calling, or perhaps he didn't think it was a gunshot, but anyhow, he started off down the driveway towards the house. That sound came again, and then again as Steve reached the trees, and then it went quiet and I lost sight of Steve. I looked across the lake, but I couldn't see the boy with the fishing pole. Behind me, Dave was telling Tino something about acoustics, how the church might be a problem.

I shivered. The light was going and it was starting to get cold.

Now Steve walked out of the trees. He was followed by another man, and the two of them stood talking in front of a rusty truck. The man was a sight. He was shirtless and covered in tattoos from his neck to his belt. I couldn't tell much more about him, except that he was wearing a red cap, but I did make out the biggest tattoo. It was a rebel flag, right across his back. He gestured towards the lake and that's when I saw it. As he dropped his arm, the flag rippled.

After a few minutes they shook hands. The man went off under the trees and Steve came up the driveway, panting a bit. As we drove away, I asked him what had happened.

"Well, we found him," he said. "That was Buckner! He's going to be fantastic. He lives in the house down there, would you believe it? I can't wait to get this on film. Right now he's busy, so—"

"What was that sound we heard?"

"He was chopping wood," Steve said. "No, sorry. He was *splitting* wood. That's what he said. He promised some for somebody, or something. I don't know. It's hard to understand him. But he'll be there tomorrow, and he wants us to come back. Which we will! We'll come back with bells on, right?"

I didn't say anything. I was watching the sun set over the tree-tops. When we reached the motel, there were already some stars. I never saw stars in London. I don't think I even looked for them. There was always too much going on around me—too many lights, too many passing cars, too many passing thoughts. Here, nothing moved except branches in the wind. A few more cars had appeared, but they were silent, each slotted in front of a room. The air was blue with night, the motel darkening. Only the office was bright, but it looked empty.

An hour later Steve knocked on my door. He wanted a drink, he said, in a hurry. I hurried out, but Steve didn't knock on the other two doors. He just stood there in the cold and dark, bouncing on the spot. I glanced at the office. It still looked empty.

"You know how great this is?" Steve said. "Do you realize? John-Boy, this is going to *make* me. It'll put me on the fucking map."

"I hope so," I said. "Shall we get a drink?"

"Absolutely," he said, but he kept bouncing up and down. "Now remember, we're still working. We can drink, but we're on the job. That's one of the perks of the job. Sometimes you *have* to go to a pub. Nose around, get information, you know? Tonight the main thing is to find interviewees, and I need your help. Tino's all over the place, and Dave's . . . well, Dave is Dave. So it's down to us. You and me. Okay?"

I don't remember what I said then, but I remember what Steve said. He went into this big pep talk, all about comfort zones and how you had to get out of them, had to test yourself, whatever that meant to you personally. In my case, it meant *talking to people*. All I had to do was go up to strangers and say hello, and brilliant things would follow. Talking to people would make stuff happen, would change my outlook, would surprise the hell out of me.

Oh yes, I remember what he said. And I remember his face in the light from the motel, that crazed look Steve gets when he becomes the Terminator. I remember it all, though I never guessed I would. At the time I was just irritated. I liked the idea of a drink. Did I really have to pay for it by hearing a lecture from my idiot brother? But I did my dance, the usual John-Boy routine. I wagged my head thoughtfully and made little thoughtful sounds, and generally pretended to listen to Steve—or that's how it seemed. Ten years later it seems quite different. Now I would say that I was pretending to myself, not Steve, because I *was* listening. As it turns out, I was all ears.

And here I have to pause. I have to give thanks again, to Steve and to God. There's no better way to put it than giving thanks, unless you call it prayer, and there's no more that I can say, in the end, than thank you, or amen. So I thank you. For that moment together in the dark and the cold, brother to brother, and for many other moments, so much else, all the beauty in my life today, I say thank you, I say amen.

Part 2

Shelby's Bar & Barbeque is gone now. Shelby died and her son took over, and he drank away the profits. The motel is still open, under the same name, but the building next door is boarded up. I pass it sometimes, and I always think of that night with Steve and Tino and Dave, the four of us shouting drunk, with music playing and people dancing, the room veiled in smoke. It was a night of many firsts. My first American beer. My first taste of barbecue. My first laugh at a southern joke. And more than that, it was the first time I began to understand where I was, began to *be* in the South.

The very first thing, as soon as we walked through the door, was all the moustaches. There was a bar down one side of the room with men ranged along it, and every one of them had a moustache. Some had beards too. Some had long beards, like Gandalf. It was funny. In London at that time, moustaches were suspiciously gay and beards were for artsy types, photographers and fashion people (unless it was a Gandalf beard, in which case you might have mental problems). These men were neither, not by a long shot. They wore blue jeans and cowboy boots and loud checked shirts, and so did the women. There were lots of women, mostly sitting at tables lined opposite the bar—couples eating and drinking. Between the bar and the tables was a wide wooden floor, with waitresses bobbing around in tight T-shirts, and beyond them, under bright lights, an empty stage.

I left the others at the bar and sat down. Immediately a waitress appeared. She had big boobs and a big red smile. "Welcome to Shelby's," she said and handed me a menu. "What you drinking?"

"I don't know," I said. "What's good?"

"Everything's good, I guess."

The menu didn't list beers, and I was scanning the bar for clues when a voice spoke behind me. "'Scuse me, buddy. You from England?"

That was how I met Bob and Doris Looney, an old couple from North Carolina. Bob Looney said he'd once been stationed in some town in Wiltshire. Did I know it? Honestly I didn't, but I decided to say yes. When I cocked my head to think about it, Bob locked eyes on me as if his life somehow hung in the balance. My answer pleased him no end. He smiled fondly at his wife, and then at me, and recommended that I order a Bud.

"You're in redneck country now," Bob said, "and Budweiser is what we drink. That or Miller. Well, any damn thing, long as it's cold. Can't stand that hot English beer. Loved the people, hated the beer."

Bob and Doris lived near the coast, where it was flat as a dollar bill. They had come to the mountains to look at the leaves, which they did every fall, and they always stayed at the Shelby Motel because it was right by this restaurant. It meant that Bob didn't have to drive after supper, which meant that he could drink. "I'm retired!" he kept saying in explanation, like it amazed him, or maybe confused him.

Doris Looney hushed her husband and told me about barbecue, which was one of those fifty-seven-variety type deals. Basically it was slow-cooked meat, pork or beef, but it was done in different ways in different states, sour in North Carolina and sweet here in Tennessee, and could be served in different ways, pulled apart or as ribs, and also came with different sides, like baked beans or coleslaw or collard greens, and you could add all sorts of things too, like vinegar or hot sauce . . . I chose a pulled pork sandwich and fries. It tasted of sugar and grease and smoke, and went perfectly with the beer, which was thin but very cold, and cut through the barbecue like mouthwash. I ordered another Bud, and then another, and then suddenly I was deep in conversation with a man called Wade Henderson.

I don't remember how the conversation began. Perhaps Wade asked if he could sit at my table, or perhaps he just sat down and I asked him about Lee Buckner. Whatever. We got talking, and I'm glad we did, because Wade told me many things I do remember. He was an older man, tall and lean, wearing overalls and heavy boots. That's what farmers often wear, and he might have been a farmer, but I don't think so. He spoke too well. Wade talked slowly but at length, with a sort of offhand attention to detail, throwing in odd remarks to prove a point or for my amusement. You could tell that he enjoyed the light shed by his own words. Maybe he was some kind of professor, or used to be. He'd certainly read a lot. I hope he reads this one day, if he's still around, which is doubtful. Wade drank the whole time we talked. Straight whiskey, shot after shot. When he'd finished saying something and his glass was empty, he'd raise one finger and another glass would appear at his elbow, and on we'd go. He drank like people smoke—like punctuation.

Wade didn't know Lee Buckner, but that's about all he didn't know. In answer to some question of mine, probably about the Cherokee, he launched into a history of the region, complete with names and dates, and several long asides on "hillbilly culture," which made his face soften with pride. I learned that the Appalachian Mountains stretched from Canada down to Georgia, and the Southern Appalachians were the highest. A few Spanish conquistadors made it over them, but the British empire stopped on the eastern flank. Here on the western side, the first pioneers set up their own government, called the Watauga Compact, and they fought like wildcats in the Revolutionary War. These people were Scots-Irish and German and English, some of them gung-ho religious, like the Quakers, and others on the run from who-knows-what. There was an old joke about the first thing a pioneer did. English pioneers built a church, Germans built a barn, and the Scots-Irish built a whiskey still. Whatever they built, they had to defend it from the Cherokee, until Andrew Jackson shuffled the Indians off to Oklahoma on the Trail of Tears. Some Cherokee remained, in remote places like the Smoky Mountains, and most people around here had some Cherokee blood. Not much colored blood, though. The slave plantations were in West Tennessee and down in the Deep South. Here it was small farms, lots of tobacco, the only cash crop—not counting moonshine, which really took off during Prohibition. Because of moonshine and what city folk considered "poverty," the hillbilly image arose. There was a grain of truth in it, back in the day, but mostly it was bullshit. Appalachian people were no more dirty and ignorant than anyone else, and they sure weren't stupid. There was no brain drain here after the Civil War, because everyone owned a bit of land, unlike the crackers farther south. No, what other Americans once called ignorance, and some still called ignorance—it was their own reflection in the mirror of their tiny minds. They had no idea of the wealth of hillbilly culture, which stood apart from the soul-sucking uniformity of modern America. The United States of emptiness. Those people, they were living in a wasteland and didn't know it. Here, folks knew where they came from, and who they were, and they *hated* being told what to do.

"We love God and family and guns," Wade said. "Maybe not in that order, and maybe not all the time, but the three things are related. That's what the liberals don't get, those humanist Yankee liberals, and all the dumbass tree huggers in California."

Wade raised a finger and glanced around, and that's when I saw Summer, the girl from the motel. She was at the bar with another girl, a blonde. They both wore tight jeans and skimpy denim jackets—identical jackets, except that the left sleeve of Summer's hung loose. Steve was talking to Summer, and the other girl was leaning forward to hear. I started to get up, but at that moment the ceiling lights dimmed.

The room quietened.

On the stage stood five men, all in white cowboy hats and all holding stringed instruments. They were clean cut and looked about my age, apart from the man in the middle, with a banjo, who was weather-beaten to an ageless brown. He tipped his hat at the crowd and spoke into a microphone.

"Howdy, folks. We're the Baileyton Bluegrass Boys, from over in Greene County. Real pleased to be here. I've heard good things about your Wednesday night pickin'. In fact, feller here told me the bands always do a great job, and have a big time, and that's what we're all looking for on this fine evening. Am I right? Let's see now. How about "Little Maggie"?

And with that, he plucked a few notes on the banjo and the band jumped in. They hit a slowish, rolling sort of groove, with the guitar player singing and the others bunched around him for the choruses. It was a sad and haunting song, a lament for little Maggie, who'd gone off with another man but didn't seem pleased about it, and was maybe contemplating some act of violence, though in a way that was curiously happy-go-lucky.

> *Last time I saw little Maggie*
> *She was sitting on the banks of the sea*
> *With a forty-four around her*
> *And a banjo on her knee*

The audience loved it. They whistled and stamped until the banjo player bent towards his mike.

"Why, thank you. That tune's a dandy, ain't it? So, how you folks doin'? I like this time of year, don't you? The cool nights, the fall leaves, geese flying south. Geese. There's a puzzling creature. Geese always fly in a V, and one side of the V is always longer than the other. Ever noticed that? Ever looked up and wondered why? Well, I'll tell you. One side of the V is longer than the other because . . . there's more geese in it!"

Everyone laughed and the band struck up another sad song, and so the evening went, with more jokes followed by more melancholy music, and a lot more drinking. Perhaps it was the effect of so much cold Bud, but the laughter and the sadness seemed to mingle as the night went on, until I felt a kind of wild joy in this wailing music—ecstasy at the summit of sadness.

Or I was just drunk, as I say.

Anyhow, I remember being strangely moved that night, even though I disliked folk music in England, especially fiddle playing, and even though the songs didn't always make sense. As the band stepped off stage for a break, Wade explained that the oldest songs were originally ballads from Britain. One of the most famous, "Knoxville Girl," started out as "The Oxford Girl." Over time the words got changed and jumbled up, and new instruments were added. The mandolin, the banjo. Did I know that the banjo came from West Africa? Slaves brought it over, along with the basic elements of the blues and . . .

Wade raised a finger.

"Well, I won't get into country music. It's a whole mess of things, all stirred together. My point is, the wellspring is right here, in these mountains. You can trace a direct line from those old ballads to Hank Williams, Johnny Cash, even Elvis."

The waitress brought another shot and I stood up, a bit unsteadily. Summer was still at the bar. Steve was now talking to her blonde friend and Summer was alone, just looking around.

Wade and I shook hands.

"Pleased to meet you, son," he said. "Thanks for listening. I talk up a storm and I know it. You take care now, and don't get none on you."

I didn't know what that meant—still don't, actually—but I wasn't about to ask. I walked towards the bar, with Summer's green eyes blazing at me.

"I didn't see you at the motel," I told her. "Thought you'd gone home."

"Oh, did you want something?"

"No, no," I said. "I'm fine. I'm more than fine."

She smiled. "Well, good."

Our eyes met and suddenly I blanked. I couldn't think of a thing to say. What a nice motel? What a nice country? What big green eyes? It was a ghastly moment, and it seemed to stretch out forever. I felt the old blackness descend on me, and I might have turned on my heels and walked out, I really might, but then she spoke.

"I did go home for an hour," she said. "I left early, but don't tell anybody. My mother was all to hell. She gets crazy about the littlest things, and calls me up and . . . It was nothing. Just a porch step is broke and needs fixing. I'll find a carpenter."

"I'm a carpenter!"

I must have said it too loudly or with too much enthusiasm, because Summer gave me a look. "You are?" she said. "I thought you were a cameraman or . . . you know, for that movie y'all are making."

Now I had plenty to say. Words came pouring out so fast that Summer laughed and slapped my shoulder.

"Slow down!" she said. "You're in the *South*. We don't do fast-talking. Now, let's start again. One thing at a time. What's your name?"

And so I explained about myself, or as much as I could in a suitably slow-talking way, how I lived in London and this was my first time in America, and Summer told me she'd love to see London, having grown up on the Mary Poppins movie, and she'd love to see other places too, like Paris and Italy and Hawaii, but she'd never been anywhere at all, apart from vacations to Myrtle Beach, partly because her daddy died and she moved back home with her mother, who wasn't coping well, and was I really a carpenter?

"I really am," I said. "Let me prove it to you."

"Are you free tomorrow afternoon?"

"I am completely free," I said, because I didn't care what Steve thought, and because I was wasted.

"Well, *okay*," Summer said. "I get off at two tomorrow. Meet me at the motel and we'll go to my house."

Then the band started up again, and now people were dancing. The music seemed to get faster and faster. I only recall the name of one song, "Freeborn Man." When the banjo player announced it, the place erupted. Soon everyone was dancing, including Steve and Tino, and even Dave, and then even me. Summer waved me onto the dance floor, so I did my best, which isn't saying a lot. Steve was surprisingly good, though. I hadn't seen him dance since he was a kid, and I'd never imagined he could do much with that oafish body. Maybe the bouncy shoes helped. Anyway, that's my last memory of the night, Steve floating around the dance floor like a fat Cupid on invisible wings.

Oh, and one other thing. I've just remembered it. When we left the bar, I saw Wade Henderson out in the parking lot. He was staggering badly. I thought he might collapse, but he made it across the asphalt and rested against an old pickup. Then he opened the door of the pickup and nearly fell backwards. That took a while. Finally he slid into the pickup and the door slammed and the lights came on. I didn't watch him drive off. I didn't even want to think about it.

———

I woke with an aching head. For a moment I thought I'd crashed my motorbike and was in hospital. Then I saw the picture on the wall. The picture showed a lion and a lamb sitting together on short grass beneath fluffy clouds. The grass was perfect, like green carpet. My father would have loved it. I imagined him sitting there with the animals, enjoying the heavenly grass, not a weed in sight.

Then Steve knocked on the door.

Outside it was bright and warm, almost hot. The other three were standing by the car, eating from paper bags. Steve handed me a bag.

"It's called a sausage biscuit," he said, "but it's not what you think. Here's coffee. You'll need it."

The "biscuit" looked like a scone without butter. It tasted like a scone without butter. But the slice of sausage tasted like sausage, and the coffee was nice and wet.

"*Bene*," Tino said, and threw his bag in a trash can. "So, Steve. Last night you meet and greet, you ask many questions. Today you have answers?"

Steve yawned. "Not really. People know about Buckner, for sure, but they're not saying what they know. Could be they're protecting him, closing ranks. A community thing, against outsiders. Or it could be that . . . maybe he's insane. Nutters make people nervous. Would you want him in your neighborhood, a man who lives like he does, and walks on water?"

"Hang on," I said. "Walks on water? You keep saying that, but you just read it in the paper. You don't know that Buckner claims anything of the sort."

"Right, I don't. That's what today is all about. We're going to put Buckner under the microscope. Let's nail that fucker till he squirms." Steve chucked his bag at the trash can and missed. "You ready?"

I hadn't even brushed my teeth, but there was no stopping the Terminator. Before I could say a word, Steve was in the car and starting the engine. Tino and Dave got in too. I picked up Steve's bag and dropped it in the trash can, and off we went.

Buckner was waiting for us. As we came down his driveway, he appeared out of the trees and waved. Steve told us he'd do the talking and I should help Dave and Tino, and I told Steve that was wonderful, honey, I love to hear you talk, and then we stopped on the dirt beside the old pickups. Steve sat there a moment, just sat there. He didn't move or speak. It was kind of odd. Then he jumped out and walked off with Buckner, and we started unpacking the equipment, which took longer than you might think. I wasn't surprised. I'd spent half my life working in film studios, and they are extremely boring places. Most of the time you stand around while some guy tries to repair a cable or something, and all the big shots, the director and the star and the star's friends, they're off in another room, laughing and eating peanuts.

When Tino and Dave were all set, we took the stuff around the side of the house to the back porch, where Steve and Buckner were sitting in rocking chairs like old friends. The porch had a great view of the lake, which was now sparkling, but the porch itself was in a state. Once it must have been handsome—wide and deep, with thick floorboards painted white. That was way back, though. Nothing had been done for years, it looked like, except to drop tools here and there, and kick some broken chairs into a corner.

Steve introduced us one by one, and we all shook hands. Lee spoke to each of us as we shook. "Howdy, how are ye?" he said, with a softness that reminded me of Summer's voice.

The man didn't look nearly as forbidding as before, and he was shorter than I'd realized—the same height as Steve but half the weight. He was a bit older than me, I thought, and maybe stronger. He had the wiry strength of a working man, though today his upper half was concealed in a loose shirt. So, no tattoos. No cap, either. His hair was dark and wild, like a little dark explosion on top of his head. But his face was clean-shaven. And his eyes were very clear, and very open. What do I mean? I mean he looked awake. Yes, that's it. Lee Buckner looked wide awake.

"Now, Steve," he said, "afore we git going, they's two thangs to discuss. First thang, I'm gonna tell you sumpin, and then I'm gonna ax you sumpin. If it don't settle right with neither of us, well then, it was good meeting you."

Steve was right about one thing. The man *was* hard to understand. Although he spoke slowly, the lilt in his voice was bigger, or bouncier, than Summer's. It made his words swoop about in ways I didn't expect. I had to concentrate, and even then I missed a few things, but what Lee said was roughly this: he didn't want to talk about walking on water, because he didn't know what it meant. He was "praying on it." When God anointed you to do something, he said, you should accept it and not *use* it. Or test it, like them snake-handling folks.

"What snake-handling folks?" Steve asked.

"Jest be happy to serve God," he said, "to be in the Spirit. Ain't nothing to talk about. Nothing to *think* about. That's how you lose yourself, if you git my meaning. Jest be happy and praise the Lord."

And he smiled.

I can't explain it, but his smile seemed to blow through me. It was a like a small gust of wind, inside. All at once my hangover disappeared. I felt fine. It was good standing there with the sun on my back, the lake sparkling, birds singing.

Steve looked down, up again, blinked. "What's the second thing?"

"It's a question," Lee said. "Do you believe in God?"

"Yes, I do," Steve said.

"How 'bout you?"

"Me?" I said. "Oh, I'm just here to help. I'm his brother, actually. These two guys are the film crew. Perhaps, er, ask them."

"I'm axing you."

I glanced at Steve, who gave a tiny shrug, which might have been a signal or might not, and either way the man was asking me and looking into my eyes and I felt the wind blow inside me and I opened my mouth.

"No, I don't believe in God," I said. "I think the world is a terrible place, full of pain. Pain and death. Where's God? I don't see God. No."

"Thank you, sir. I appreciate your honesty."

I nodded.

Lee turned to Steve. "All right then. Where you wanna do this?"

They decided to do it right there, on the back porch, since the light was good and Dave liked the acoustics. While Tino set up the tripod and Dave fiddled with the clip mike, Steve produced the life rights consent agreement. He gave it to Lee, who held it close to his face, page after page, and finally signed it. Then Dave attached the clip mike to Lee's shirt and Steve clapped in front of Lee's face. That was a nice moment. Lee was so startled he almost went over backwards in the rocking chair. Steve had to calm him down. He explained that the clap was a marker, so they could synchronize the sound with the film. It was called a sync clap.

"Well, don't do it agin," Lee said, and we all laughed.

That was how the interview began, with laughter, but it ended differently. I don't like to think about it, even now, and I'm not going to give you a blow-by-blow of the whole event. Watch Steve's film. Most of it's there. No, I'll give you a short version, my version, which is the truth.

Steve started with basic questions—where Lee was from, and so on—and then Steve stopped talking, because Lee embarked on the story of his life. He was born and raised in Mountain City, Tennessee (which he pronounced *Tina-see*). His father was a builder and taught Lee the trade, but Lee hadn't seen him in years. The old man was long gone, maybe dead, and his mother was somewhere in Georgia or Alabama, maybe married. Early on, Lee got into drugs. Crack cocaine, crystal meth. He said, "And always, night 'n' day, he was in the mountains and in the tombs, a-cryin' and a-cuttin' hisself with stones. Mark 5:5. That was me." At the age of twenty-three he lost his mind and shot up a convenience store in Majestic, Kentucky. The judge gave him ten years, and Lee did ten years. When he left the joint he was clean but homeless. Lee's half-brother, Ryan, took him in. Ryan and his wife lived in a trailer park within earshot of Bristol Motor Speedway, the famous NASCAR track. They gave Lee a room, a pile of T-shirts left by someone, and a Dodge pickup that "kindly went along." Lee was grateful. He found yard work in a new subdivision beside a golf course, and soon he'd saved enough to buy an old riding mower and had several regular customers. One of his customers was an old lady who lived alone, and they became friends. She told him about Jesus Christ, how he passed from death unto life, and she said that everybody could pass from death unto life if they listened to the words of Jesus: "Ye must be born again." And she gave him a Bible, the same Bible he used today.

Here I got confused. I may have missed something that Lee said, or *he* may have missed something, perhaps intentionally. I remember that he paused. Anyway, he had a fight with his brother, who was looking to kill him, so he needed to get out of Tennessee. At the probation office he ran into an old cellmate, who offered him five hundred bucks to go on a drug run to Florida. A bunch of people were putting money in, and all Lee had to do was drive down to this pain clinic, where the guy had a connection, and pick up the drugs. So Lee went. He drove down to some place in South Florida and parked at Burger King, behind the pain clinic. He sat there and waited, and someone came up to his truck, but it wasn't the person he was supposed to meet. It wasn't a person at all. It was an angel of the Lord. The angel got into Lee's truck and spoke to him without speaking, and then got out of the truck and walked away. Now Lee knew what to do. The purpose of his life was clear as a bell. He left the parking lot and drove to Vistaprint, where he spent the drug money on two thousand leaflets titled *SAY HELLO TO JESUS CHRIST!* He handed these leaflets to everybody, everywhere, sleeping in his truck and going where the Lord told him to go—north most of the time—until the Lord led him here.

"To East Tennessee," Steve said.

"Right here," Lee said. "This very spot."

The house and barn had belonged to an old mechanic, a widower without kids. The man was about to move to a nursing home, and that's when Lee came driving down the road. The man gave him everything. Ten acres. The land up behind the barn, that was all tobacco once upon a time. Now it was "growed up." But the barn was still good. First thing he did was make a pulpit. He had to do some repairs too, but he worked with what he had, or what was given. Last month a junkyard in Buladean gave him two windows and a high-dollar front door, as a love offering, and he'd just hung the door, only the hinges didn't seem—

"Wait a minute," Steve said. "You're driving along and meet this old guy, and he says, here you are, it's all yours? Why? Why'd he do it?"

"I guess the Lord moved him to do it."

"And that was when?"

"Five ears? Six ears ago."

"So you turned the barn into a church, right? Don't you need some kind of approval to set up your own church?"

"Where they's two or three gathered in my name, there am I in the midst 'em. Matthew 18:20."

"Well, okay. But to *run* a church you need qualifications. Ministers are ordained. They've been through training."

"Trainin'?" Lee smiled. "I been through trainin'. My whole life is trainin'. Never stops. Son, if you wanna be a pastor, you need to love God, to let him into your heart. You need to be *saved*. Jesus will do the rest."

Steve scratched his head. He literally scratched his head. That bit is not in the film. Nor is what happened next, though it should be. For me, the best moment came now, when Steve asked Lee how he knew what to say. Did he just stand at the pulpit and say what he felt?

"What I feel ain't important," Lee said. "It teetotally ain't. What is important is the words of Jesus Christ. I preach the New Testament and only that. Fact, I had a mind to call my church the New Testament Church, but I seen it was the Devil tempting me. The Devil loves a division. Anything to git folks arguing, specially over the Bible. No, this church is nondenominational. It's jest a church of God. It's open to ever'body, and it's always open, simple as that."

Lee went silent. Then he looked at me and said this:

"I'll tell you sumpin else. I don't understand the Old Testament. I don't understand it, so I let it alone. I ain't a smart feller. Look at all the stupid thangs I done! But I love Jesus. And Jesus don't care 'bout smarts, or where you been, what you done. He cares what you do today, tomorrow, the rest of your life. Listen to the Lord. Listen to him. Jest listen to him."

There was a pause then, filled with birdsong. I don't know what kind of bird it was, but its music spoke to me. Then a motorbike went past, a big one, and its engine spoke to me. The sunlight spoke to me too. It spoke without speaking.

Steve's film cuts in at this point, although you can't hear the bird. I suppose the clip mike didn't pick it up. But it picked up Steve, very clearly.

"Lee, I want to know something. Did you walk on water? I've heard that you walked on water, more than once. Did you do it? Did you?"

Lee looked away at the lake.

"You see, I'd really like to film you walking on water. Would you consider doing that?"

Lee unclipped the mike, gave it to Steve and stood up. "You have a nice day, gentlemen," he said, and went into the house.

———

We ate barbecue again for lunch, but I didn't enjoy it as much today. The atmosphere must have affected the food. It was too quiet. There were only a few others in the bar, and Steve was pissed off. He'd hardly spoken since we left Buckner's. Now Steve held up a french fry and gazed at it. He turned it slowly in his fingers, as if contemplating the mystery of french fries.

"I don't get it," he said. "I just don't get it."

"What did you expect?" I said. "He told you not to ask him, he made a big deal about it, and then you asked him!"

"Because he *wanted* to be asked. That's *why* he made a big deal. It's a game. Celebrities do it to reporters all the time. Close you down, open up. The bottom line is that everyone's dying to be on camera, to be seen doing their thing, *including* holy people. They might play harder to get, but they still want to be got. Otherwise how are they going to spread their message? Look at the pope, the Dalai Lama. If Jesus was alive today he'd have a PR person, one of the disciples. Another disciple would be his YouTube guy. Mary Magdalene would do Facebook. You know?"

Steve wagged the french fry at me, then ate it.

I said, "No, I don't know. You're just making stuff up. It doesn't prove anything. The fact is, Buckner's not like that."

"Then why did he walk on water? Why'd he do it if he didn't want attention? What was the point?"

"Maybe there isn't a point," I said. "Maybe he *thinks* he walked on water. He thinks it, but really he was . . . sleepwalking?"

Tino looked at Steve, who sat back and looked at all of us, and then shook his head. Steve said, "He did more than think about it.

Something happened. I have a gut feeling. Whatever it was, and however he did it, *something happened* and *somebody saw it happen*. Ah, fuck it. Let's go to Johnson City. We need to find that journalist. At least *she'll* be happy to talk to us."

That was when I announced my plan for the afternoon. I'd expected a fight with Steve, especially in this mood, but he liked the idea. For some reason it cheered him up. He said I should take some clearance forms, in case I came across good interviewees, and he handed me a small camera.

"Keep it," he said. "I brought another one as backup. These digital cameras are getting cheap, and they're good quality. They even do a bit of video."

"But what it's for?"

"Prep work," Steve said. "Anything that strikes you, that makes you stop and look. Show it to Tino. We're making a *film*, remember?"

———

Just before two, fresh from a shower, I left my room and saw Summer across the parking lot. She was standing by a long white car, the kind of gas-guzzler you see in seventies movies. As I walked over, she dropped a cell phone in her bag and said, "Hi."

"Hi," I said. "Nice ride."

She looked at the car. "It was my daddy's. He loved these big old Fords. You wanna go?"

Summer talked slow but she drove fast, and with surprising ease. She held the steering wheel loosely at three o'clock, spinning it this way and that as the road twisted upwards. From where I sat, I couldn't see the empty left sleeve of her blouse, and I soon forgot about it. There was so much else on my mind. The flickering woods. Splashes of light and sudden long views, mountains lost in haze. Summer's beautiful laugh. She told me she'd just been texting Kendra—"My friend? From last night?"—who thought my brother had been hitting on her, and I said that if she had to think about it then he wasn't, because Steve had the subtlety of a hammer, and Summer burst out laughing. I hadn't seen a woman laugh so loudly for a long time, unless she was faking it. Summer wasn't faking, not in the least. This was a hundred-percent laugh, a tip-your-head-back, eyes-and-mouth laugh. It was a laugh that stayed with you, that you kept.

When Summer had recovered, I asked if she had any Cherokee in her, and she said, "Because of the hair?"

"And the cheekbones."

"My great-grandfather was a full-blooded Cherokee. His wife was Irish. I mean she was born in Ireland. My daddy always said she had the bluest eyes, and that was why his momma had green eyes, like me. Brown and blue makes green, according to Daddy. He said that if I married a blue-eyed man, we might get violet. My daddy was full of crazy notions."

"And are you married?" I asked, because I had to ask, even though it hadn't occurred to me before.

"I was," she said. "And he had blue eyes. Troy had real blue eyes. But my daughter's eyes are like mine."

"Daughter? Really? You have a daughter?"

Summer glanced at me. "I'm twenty-seven. It ain't a big surprise. Yeah, I have Deedee. She's seven now. She was four when I threw Troy out. You wanna hear about it? I'll tell you if you like. I don't care."

I didn't take in all the details, but I learned that Summer used to work at Food City in Boone, and that Troy became addicted to OxyContin, a prescription drug known as "hillbilly heroin." Troy usually fetched Deedee from day care, since he wasn't working much, but one afternoon he didn't show. The day care called Summer, who called Kendra, who picked up Deedee and kept her for a few hours, then brought her home. This was July. A warm evening, still light. Summer pulled in at the same time as Kendra and found Troy lying in the front yard—in the middle of the front yard, on his side. She just knew he was dead.

But he wasn't. He was asleep.

When she woke him up, he hit her.

"It flew all over me," Summer said. "And then I went somewhere else. I don't remember it, but Kendra says I beat the tar out of Troy. Evidently I lit into him and didn't stop till he got in his truck. I remember that. I stood by the truck and cussed him out, called him everything but a white boy."

"Why's that?"

"Why's what?"

"Why didn't you call him a white boy? Was he black?"

"Black with blue eyes? No, Troy's white." She sighed. "I'm sorry. It's a dumb expression. I ain't prejudiced, I really ain't."

"Your language is," I said, and I couldn't believe that I was saying it, that I was taking such a risk. But what was I risking? I thought I was risking Summer's respect for me, which I was, but I was also risking my respect for her. I was risking both of us, in each other's eyes, for the sake of the moment, and the day, and maybe days to come. I see that now. I see it with enormous clarity, as if I were holding this moment up to the light—like Steve holding up the french fry, turning it slowly, noticing the angles.

Thank God, Summer took it well.

"It's the language, not me," she said. "You can't avoid it living in the South. We shouldn't even say 'black.' My daughter says 'African American.' And *you*, you should call me an 'Appalachian American.'" She smiled. After a few seconds she said, "I guess language is a kind of history, a living history."

She was right. I'd never thought of that. It reminded me of my conversation with Wade Henderson, and I said, "Like music."

Summer smiled again. "Like music."

Now we hit a level stretch without houses. Trees overhung the road on both sides, scattering the sunlight, so that we seemed to glide down a long twinkling corridor. At the end of the corridor was a big green sign with a flag.

"Welcome to North Carolina," I said. "We're going to North Carolina?"

"We are," she said, "and *now* we're in North Carolina."

The road dropped through trees and then we shot out into an empty meadow beneath an empty sky. Beyond us were mountains, a world of mountains. The scale was hard to grasp. The more I stared into the distance, the less distance I saw, until I lost perspective on the mountains near us. They didn't even look like mountains. They looked soft and airy, like great piles of blue dust.

"Wow," I said. Then I said it again, and then I felt silly, so I said something else. "Can I ask you a question, a personal question? What happened to your arm?"

"Nothing happened to it," she said. "I never had a left arm. I was born like this."

"Oh."

And that was that.

We dropped through trees again, down and down, in a series of tight switchbacks with little margin for error—only a foot of asphalt beyond the white line. Summer braked on the curves, but not much. If anything, she drove faster downhill. Even on a motorbike I couldn't have kept up with her, and I was glad when we sailed into a valley dotted with barns. I saw a big red barn, a green one, a black one, and then Summer turned down a gravel driveway beside a creek. The driveway ended at a white two-story house. On either side were low wooden buildings, also painted white, and in front was a hammock strung between two fruit trees.

Before we'd stopped, a dark-haired girl slid out of the hammock, fell over, picked herself up and came running towards us.

Summer hugged her daughter, who looked up at me with big green eyes. Then a woman appeared on the porch and tripped down the steps. She jumped the last step and marched across the grass to meet us. I knew immediately that I had to be on best behavior—sometimes you just know. Summer introduced her mother, Madge, who crossed her arms and glared at me.

"I'm Margaret," she said. "Margaret is my name."

I said that I was a carpenter and I'd come all the way from England to help her, which had no effect on the woman. She stayed exactly as she was, glaring, with her thin arms crossed, until Summer led me over to the porch. The bottom step was rotted. I asked Summer about tools and she said, "In the shop."

"Shop? You have a . . . store?"

"*Workshop*," she said. "Over there. That other building is the sawmill. Daddy built it first, then cut the lumber to build the shop. He also built the porch, I think, but my grandfather built the house."

The workshop was dark and dusty, and had a particular smell. It was a mixture of damp and sawdust, with a hint of something else, perhaps something beyond smell—a sense of silence. As I peered at the workbenches, Summer told me her daddy had died two years ago, in a farming accident. He fell off his tractor, somehow. She reckoned he'd been drinking, but Momma didn't want to hear that. Now they leased their fields to a neighbor, a good man who paid them more than he had to, but the man didn't go to church, and his sons were wild, and Momma . . . well, Momma was still grieving, but she didn't want to hear that either, and did I need to look in the sawmill?

I found a plank—in fact, lots of planks—and trimmed it with a circular saw, and cut it to length, and rebuilt the porch step. It didn't take thirty minutes. When I was done, I stood on the step and said, "Voila!" I doubt that Summer's mother had ever heard anyone say "Voila!" But she ignored my strange oath and tested the step herself, and this did have an effect on her. She nodded to herself. Then she laid a hand on my arm, very gently, and asked if I'd like some lemonade.

We sat on the porch in the afternoon sun, while Deedee showed Summer what she could do with a hula hoop, which wasn't much, and Margaret scolded her granddaughter for various things, like stepping in a flower bed and pushing down her sweatpants.

"Deedee, pull up your britches!" she said.

Britches. I remember that so well. It sounded like Shakespeare, and it triggered something inside me. Suddenly I had the dreamiest feeling. It was the sun too, the way it shone gold over the plowed fields and the barns and the little creek, giving it all a fairytale glow, as if I'd wandered into a Disney movie about ye olde days, before machines took over, when people spoke like Shakespeare and painted their barns different colors and drank lemonade as the sun went down . . . Movies again. I couldn't escape them, couldn't see beyond them, even though I knew, I *knew,* they were blinding me to the world. Because movies aren't how the world is. Disney doesn't show beautiful young women with one arm, or fathers who die in farming accidents because they're drunk, or husbands who take pills and beat their wives. That's the world, whatever else the world may be. Life is not a dream. *We* are the dream, with all our glowing ideas about life. Like movies, we flash and fade.

Anyway, we sat on the porch.

After an hour or so, Summer said she'd take me back to the motel. Her mother offered to pay me for my work, and I said no, it was a pleasure, and she touched my arm again and said, "Bless you."

As we drove away, I asked Summer if her mother was religious.

"Southern Baptist," she said. "Hellfire and brimstone. Momma's not as bad as some, though. You know those people who just can't wait to die? So they can be with Jesus? They're cuckoo."

"Do you go to church?"

"Sometimes, with Momma. If she wants to take Deedee, I'll go along. I like it fine. I mean, I believe, but I don't go on about it like . . . Hey! See that house up on the hill? That's where Goose lives. Goose saw Lee Buckner walk on water. So I heard. Wanna talk to him?"

It wasn't what I'd call a house. It was a small cabin, like something pictured in a storybook (or a Disney movie). The walls were made of horizontal timbers, with plaster in the chinks, and the porch roof was held up by tree trunks, actual tree trunks, with knobs where branches had been sawn off. To complete the picture, the cabin had a rock chimney running up one side, and the chimney was smoking!

As we came up the driveway, a man got to his feet and raised a hand. He was a big man, in overalls, with a straw hat pushed back on his head. He looked pretty old and pretty hardy.

"Goose is his name?" I said.

"Nickname," she said. "'Cause his last name is Gosnell, I guess."

That made no sense to me, but I let it go because we'd arrived. Summer pulled up beside a vintage jeep, complete with camouflage, as if it had just driven out of World War II. I was admiring the jeep when Summer pushed me forward.

"Goose, this here's John. He flew all the way from England."

"Flew from England?" Goose said from the porch. "Hoowee! Your arms must be tired. Better set down, son, take a load off. You'uns thirsty? Y'anna sody pop?"

Or something like that. I don't honestly know what he said. I could only catch one word in three, and he didn't catch *anything* I said. Summer had to translate in both directions, and even then it was hard work, because her translations sometimes needed translating. At one point Goose grinned at me and shook his head. He said, "Who's got the accent, you or me?"

But then, gradually, I tuned in to Goose speak. I also changed the way I spoke. I tried to phrase things as Summer would, and tried to slow down. "Tried to slow down." That's like saying, tried to relax—if you're trying, you're not relaxing. The only way to do it is really relax, really slow down. So I did.

And here's what Goose told me, more or less:

The year before, in the summer, his riding mower tore up. He worked on it, but the job took a while because it was smothering hot, and then it poured with rain. The grass grew. It got long, and long grass is snaky. So Goose called up a feller he knew, Charlie Spears. Charlie worked on small machines and always had old mowers sitting around, and Goose asked if he could borrow one. Charlie said sure thing, but he was going to Greensboro next day to visit with his daughter, which shocked the hell out of Goose because Charlie never went anywhere. Charlie said no problem, though. He'd leave the mower in the backyard and Goose could come get it any time he had a mind to. Of course, Goose ran down there in the morning, early, but Charlie had left already. Now, Charlie lived right on the lake—not in a big fancy house, but a nice place. As Goose was getting the mower onto his trailer, something caught his eye. It was real misty out on the water, but he swore he could see a man walking. The man stopped about fifty feet from Goose and looked at him, just looked at him, and then he turned and vanished into the mist.

"How'd you react?" I asked.

"Say what?"

"What did you do?"

"I come unglued."

"And you're sure it was a person? How are your eyes?"

"My eyes are good. If my knees was good, I'd go hunting. I can't climb up into a deer stand. Can't sit in one neither, not for three hours like I used to could. But my eyes are fine, son. It was a man I seen on the water, and I know the name of that man. Lee Buckner. I seen him a time or two, before and after. He lives down the road from Charlie."

"Did you tell anybody about this?"

"I told friends."

"But you didn't report it?"

"Report it? To who? The police?"

"So you didn't talk to newspapers or TV stations? You didn't tell the story to . . . anyone else? Why?"

"No one asked me."

I took a photo of Goose standing on his porch, and I gave him a clearance form, for what it was worth—not much, I'd say. The photo was worth it, though. I kept it, and still have it. Goose is a little blurred, because he was spitting tobacco juice, but then, that's how I remember Goose, a little blurred. It was so hard to understand each other, and I'd already had an eventful day.

After we said goodbye, Summer asked if I wanted to drive, and I said, "Can I?"

"Well, can you?"

"I suppose I can," I said.

I liked driving the long white Ford. It turned with a terrific sweep, as I imagined a speedboat would turn. And I liked having Summer beside me, talking and laughing, as our speedboat rode the mountain waves. It felt funny driving on the wrong side of the road, but then I realized it wasn't wrong, it was just different, and all I had to do was relax into it—not try to relax, really relax.

Part 3

The making of Steve's film, and Steve's many thoughts about his film, didn't interest me much. I had my own thoughts. In my memory, these thoughts loom so large that they practically eclipse Steve. What he did over the next few days, morning to night, I'm not certain. What happened to me, or happened inside me, that I can tell you. I want to tell you. It's part of the reason I've been sitting here in the early mornings, typing away at this laptop.

When Summer dropped me at the motel, the other three were in Steve's room. The door was wide open, but the room smelled of feet. It was a mess in there. Steve's stuff was scattered over the floor and on both chairs, everywhere but the bed. That's where they were, sitting gloomily in a row, Dave and then Steve and Tino at the end. They looked like the three bears without their own beds.

Their day hadn't gone well. They found the journalist who wrote the piece about Buckner, and she phoned the fisherman who'd told her the story, but the man's wife answered and said he was in the hospital. He'd just had a stroke and couldn't talk.

"Unbe-fucking-lievable," Steve said. "And that was pretty much it, apart from a short interview. We did it there in her office, just basic questions, chit-chat about southern fundamentalists. One thing came up, though. There are these people in Newport who handle snakes. Poisonous snakes. In church. And some of them drink poison too. Strychnine! They drink it and praise Jesus, because Jesus is the antidote to all poisons. Now, that's hardcore. Compared to this lot, Buckner is Pentecostal Lite. Those are her words, and she should know. She's from Newport. It's some little town near here. What d'you think? Might be worth checking out."

"Why?" I said. "It's nothing to do with the film."

"What film? *The Man Who Refused to Walk on Water?* Who wants to see that?"

But then I told them about meeting Goose, and I showed them my photo. Immediately the Terminator came back to life. And Tino liked the photo. Dave did too. Dave was so impressed that he actually spoke. What he said, and it's the only thing I remember him saying, were these words of wisdom: "Snakes are bleedin' dangerous. You don't wanna mess with snakes, in a church or anywhere else. I vote we film this bloke."

So they filmed Goose next morning. I did the driving and made the introductions, but I didn't go into Goose's cabin with them. I don't know why. Perhaps it was too small for all of us. Anyhow, I walked around outside and inspected the cabin, partly just to keep warm. The weather had turned again and clouds hung in the treetops. I soon forgot about the cold, though. That cabin was a master class in carpentry. I couldn't find a single nail or bolt. The whole structure held together purely by virtue of its design, plus a few wooden pegs at critical joints. Tobacco barns used to be built the same way. They're disappearing now, especially the big ones, because few people still grow tobacco, but those old barns are the cathedrals of Appalachian carpentry. Someone should write a book about them, someone who's built them and knows what they're talking about, which isn't me.

After leaving Goose, we drove to Lee Buckner's house. I've no idea what Steve had planned, though he probably told me. But it doesn't matter. Buckner wasn't there, and neither was his truck. Tino shot some "cutaways" of the lake, in case they were needed later, and Dave recorded "buzz tracks" for the same reason, I think. Steve didn't do anything, just paced in circles and then said we should go, at which point we must have returned to the motel.

I know that because I bought two barbecue sandwiches and ate them with Summer.

She was alone in the office. Nobody walked in, and the phone didn't ring. We talked for a long time, me leaning on the counter and her tipped back in an office chair. I told her about my ex, how she'd vamoosed with the TV producer and I moved in with my parents, which was humiliating at thirty-five, and Summer said she knew all about that. Here she was, a grown woman, a mother, still living with her own mother—or her mother was living with her. And we talked about other things. Summer was really into hiking, she said, and this area was famous for its mountain trails. Some of them were Indian. Daniel Boone might have used them. She drew maps of her favorite trails, including one to a waterfall and another, very steep, that led to a beautiful bald.

"What's bald?"

"That's the name. A bald is a grassy place on top of a mountain. People used to put their cows up there in summer, and they'd have family picnics. Momma talks about it, how divine it was. The cows kept the grass down, you see, which ain't the case now. Now the mountains are *protected*. They're supposed to be *natural*, whatever that means. Ain't we part of nature? Momma hates the Forest Service, calls 'em a bunch of eggheads."

Summer grinned and blinked her green eyes, and I thought, *I love you*. It just came to me. Like a voice. *I love you*.

"Can I tell you something?" I said. "I haven't told this to anybody, but I was contemplating suicide. That's what people say, isn't it? Contemplating. Like it's a decision. I don't think it's that at all, or not until the very last moment, maybe, when the decision makes itself. Suddenly you're done. You've reached the end. That's all, folks."

Her eyes stayed on me as I spoke, and then stayed after I spoke, each of us looking at the other in a deep well of silence that seemed to expand beyond the room, out into the silent parking lot, the silent trees, the silent sky.

"Don't do it, John. Please don't do it."

"No, I won't," I said. "I don't want to. I don't even know why I said that. Let's change the subject . . . Hiking. I'd like to go hiking. Tomorrow's Saturday. Are you off?"

"I'm off all weekend, but I'm taking Momma to see her sister in Nashville. We're going this afternoon."

"Can you go another time? We're flying back on Tuesday, which only leaves Monday and—"

"They planned it months ago, and Momma don't like to drive. I'm sorry, I really am."

"Me too," I said. "Me too."

What could I do?

———

I walked to the waterfall on my own. It was another cold day, with spitting rain. The rain didn't touch me though, because the trail stayed in the trees. It began near the motel and wound uphill, crisscrossing the same creek, and ended at a wide pool. Above the pool, glittering against slabs of black rock, were the white veins of the waterfall. It went up and up, higher than the trees, and the trees were huge. Vines hung down as thick as the branches, which made me think of monkeys, stupidly, but that reminded me about bears. Summer had said to watch for them. If I met a bear, I should stand my ground and see what happened. See what happened? As my mother would say, famous last words.

The next day, Sunday, was even colder. I wore my leather jacket but wished I'd brought something smarter, because we went to church. I needn't have worried. Buckner's congregation were casual dressers. There were fifteen of them, mostly older people, and one very old—a plump woman in a wheelchair. She might have been more than plump, actually, but the person behind her confused my sense of scale. Pushing the wheelchair was a young man the size of a weather balloon. He was the largest human I've ever seen standing up, if you call it standing. The wheelchair clearly served two purposes.

Inside, the church was shadowy dark—because it was a barn, of course, and also both entrances had been sealed. The only light came from two low windows with fake leading. Looking up, I saw great beams disappearing into blackness, and a few tiny spots of daylight, like stars.

Lee Buckner was sitting on a low platform, beside a tall wooden box. His pulpit, I guessed. He nodded to us and looked away. I sat down with Steve and Tino, leaving Dave at the back with the boom mike. They'd decided to record audio only, to be sensitive, though I didn't see what difference that made. I'd suggested asking permission, and Steve said he had permission: the signed consent agreement.

Now Lee stood and spread his arms.

"Welcome y'all," he said. "Oh welcome, beloved."

He called us "beloved" over and over, and told us to "listen, beloved" because he had "wunnerful news." It wasn't what I'd expected. In all the movies, backwoods churches are filled with shouting and singing, but Lee never raised his voice. He just stood in the twilight of the old barn and spoke about the parables of Jesus. I recognized some of them, vaguely. The others *were* news to me. Mysterious news. He said something about a king with ten thousand men, and that was related to the savor of salt and the building of a tower, all of which went over my head. But then he picked up a Bible and read from it. "If any man come to me, and hate not his father, and mother, and wife, and children, and brethren, and sisters, yea, and his own life also, he cannot be my disciple. Luke 14:26."

He said it so gently. You could tell he didn't hate anyone. Then he started to cry.

I cried too, though I hid it from Steve.

Lee asked us to pray with him, and he mentioned several friends who were suffering, one from emphysema and another from loneliness, and then he produced a coffee can and handed it to someone at the front. Each person put money in the can and passed it to the next person and got up and walked out. Tino put in five dollars. Steve took the five out and put in ten. I put in more than ten, but I won't say how much.

I'm not sure if Lee came outside. Steve persuaded several people to do interviews on the spot, so I was busy with the clearance forms. The last interviewee was the old woman in the wheelchair, who turned out to be charming. She joked about my pale skin and gave me a big green apple. Her grandson had picked it that morning, she said, and she'd put it in her purse and brought it to church, because she knew that someone would enjoy a nice apple, and that someone was me. Then she told Steve that Buckner was a prophet, a modern-day prophet in the wilderness, and that she believed he had the power to heal the sick. He'd walked on water, so why not this? Buckner hadn't tried it yet, but she hoped he would lay hands on her grandson, who was battling diabetes.

Her grandson was the weather balloon. He had a squeaky voice and laughed a lot. When Steve asked him what he thought of Lee Buckner, he said, "Oh, he's good. He's real good. You see him cry? Yeah, he's a crier. But he's good. Ain't he good, beloved?" And he gave a squeaky laugh.

After that, the other three drove off somewhere, maybe to eat. I walked down the road until I came to a tree with a red circle on it. The trail to the grassy bald began here, according to Summer's map. "RED PAINT ON TREE," she'd written, and drawn a vertical arrow upwards.

Her map was accurate. That trail went straight up the mountain. What with all the rocks and tree roots, and the endless thickets of laurel (which Summer called "roughs," for good reason), it took me three hours to get to the top. But I'm glad I did. Just as I clambered up through the last trees, the sun came out. I felt its heat and stopped to catch my breath, and then I saw where I was. Before me lay a broad green meadow ringed by misty peaks and brilliant bursts of cloud. It looked like a TV ad I'd worked on earlier that year, but without the naked woman holding a bottle of shampoo, and all the people milling around the studio, and all the other people outside in the streets, milling around and yammering on their phones. There was just this, there was just me.

I sat in the grass and ate the apple I'd been given, and I thought about my life, and about Summer. Green apple, green grass, green eyes. That picture often returns to me, especially in dreams. It must be down deep. I imagine that when I die it'll be among the last things to go, along with the sound of my mother's voice and the silence of English rain.

I don't know how long I sat there, but at some point I realized that I didn't feel sad, or angry, or jealous, or excited, or anything else. I didn't feel good or bad. I was . . . peaceful. That's the only word for it. My sadness and anger hadn't left me, and would probably never leave, nor would jealousy and excitement and all the rest, but now I understood that, and I was at peace with it. Because the hell that I carried with me *was* me. But that didn't mean I was in hell. It meant I was beginning to see through myself, to see the world around me, and what I saw was the hand of God.

Does that touch you in any way? Does it even make sense to you? As I say it, the moment slips away from me, and I have to close my eyes and recapture it. Let me try again. I'll put it as simply as I can.

I went up the mountain and sat in the grass and ate an apple. Nothing happened at all, on the outside, except that the sun came out. But the sun also came out inside me. Remember what I said about laughter? I said laughter is a ripple of light from above, a parting of the dark seas, a glimpse of forever. That's how it was. It was like laughter.

———————

I came down the mountain in the last thin sunshine. It was hard on the knees and I had to watch my step, so I almost missed the man on the rock. About halfway down, in a clearing above the lake, a man sat cross-legged on a mossy boulder, leaves drifting around him. He had his back to me and his head bent forward, but I thought I recognized him, and then I was sure of it. I saw the dark explosion of hair.

"Hello, Lee," I said. "Am I disturbing you?"

He slipped down from the rock and shook my hand.

"Howdy," he said. "I was jest reading my Bible. You ain't disturbing me one bit. I'm happy to see ye, John. Airish, ain't it?"

"Sorry?"

"Cold," he said. "It's getting cold. You been up on the mountain?"

I told him what I'd been doing and how much I'd enjoyed it, but that didn't begin to describe the experience, so I went into more detail, a lot more. I don't recall what I said. Even as I was speaking, the words seemed to fade like smoke, and I couldn't tell if any of them reached Lee. He stood very still, watching me, until I finally shut up. Then he nodded and said, "I hear ye."

"Oh, man," I said. "I'm rabbiting."

"Say what?"

"Talking too much."

"No, no," he said. "You're jest a-talkin' and I'm jest a-listenin'. Now you can listen and I'll talk. Jesus, he went up a mountain. D'you know it? Okay, I'll tell you. It was a high mountain, and on top of it God spoke to Jesus. He spoke out of a cloud and Jesus was revealed to the disciples. The Bible says transfigured. Jesus was transfigured before 'em, and his face did shine as the sun, and his raiment was white as the light. Matthew 17:2."

"Really?" I said.

"Really," he said.

I gazed at the lake. From up here, the water looked smooth and strangely solid, like a dark pool of wax spread through the trees.

"They call it Watauga Lake," Lee said, "but it ain't a lake. It's a reservoir. They's a whole system of reservoirs running to the Tennessee River. They drop 'em in winter. This one drops 'bout ten feet. You go out in a boat, you can look down and see houses. That's the old town of Butler."

Both of us were quiet then, facing the lake. It was an easy quiet, the kind that goes on until someone feels like breaking it.

"John, I've a mind to pray. Will you pray with me?"

"Well . . . all right."

"What's your name?"

"My last name? Mallory."

As the leaves fell around us, red and yellow, catching the sun, Lee bowed his head and I bowed mine, and he gave this short prayer:

"Lord, please holp this man, John Mallory. Holp him find his way. Guide him and comfort him and bring him to ye. Save him, Lord. That's what I'm axing. Please save John Mallory. He's an honest feller, and a real nice feller, and I'm a-gettin' to like him, Lord, and I thank you for this day. It's been a good 'un. Amen."

Lee raised his head and looked at me, and a smile came into his eyes. I felt that wind blow through me, and I smiled too. Then he walked over to the rock. He came back with something in his hand.

"John, this is for you. It's a red-letter Bible. That means the words of Jesus are in red. If I was you, I'd start with Jesus. Start with Jesus and end with Jesus. Oh yeah! There's the recipe for a sweet life."

"Is that your Bible? Didn't someone give it to you? No, Lee. I mean, thank you, but I can't accept that."

"Sure you can. They's beaucoups of Bibles. I got plenty others."

"But it's important to you."

"It *was* important to me. Now it'll be important to you. Please, John, take it."

I took it.

———

"It's a reservoir? And they drop it? In winter they drop it?"

"That's what he said."

"They bloody *drop* it!"

"So what?"

"Why didn't you tell me? And why did *he* tell you?"

"He just told me, and I didn't think you'd be interested."

"Interested? John, what the fuck? I'm a journalist. I'm following a story. *Everything* interests me."

It was late afternoon and we were sitting in Steve's room. They'd spent the day doing "admin," as Steve called it, which basically involved labeling tapes and cans of film, and arguing about what went with what. I'd been trying to catch Summer alone. Each time I walked past the office I saw this little white-haired woman in a flowery dress. She was either on the phone or waving a finger in the air. Summer acted like she was waving a knife. She seemed to be backing away.

Now Steve stood up and started kicking clothes around. He found his bouncy shoes, tightened the Velcro straps and headed for the door.

"Come on, you lot," he said. "We're going to see Buckner. He's beginning to crack, I think, or maybe he's playing with us. That's okay. We can play too. Let's give this one last shot. Tino and Dave, you better be ready. This is action stations. We're going in hot."

So we all piled into the car and set off for Lee's house. Steve drove fast. It seemed like we got there in five minutes. As we came down the driveway, Lee walked out from the trees around the house. His chest was bare and he was holding an ax. He leaned the ax against a tree and watched us come.

We crossed the yard like soldiers, Steve walking point, Tino behind aiming the camera, and Dave and me in the rear lugging equipment. We stopped about ten feet from Lee, who folded his tattooed arms across his tattooed chest. For a moment no one spoke. The only sound was that bird I'd heard before. It seemed to be right above us, singing its heart out.

"Well, Lee, we're leaving tomorrow," Steve said. "I've been thinking, and I'd like to make you a proposition. If you let us film you walk on water, we'll do it however you say. You decide where the camera goes. Put it anywhere. A hundred yards away, if you want. And we won't zoom in. No close-ups, I promise. I also promise that people will see the film and be amazed, and you'll spread the word of Christ. You'll be doing God's work. What d'you say?"

Lee didn't say anything, just stared.

"Look, I understand what you're doing. You're changing peo-ple's lives through the power of belief. Can you really walk on water? Who's to know? And what's the difference, as long as peo-ple *believe* it?"

Lee didn't blink.

"How about if we put down the camera? Go off record? It'll be just between us. Is there something you'd like to say? Now is the time, before we go. I don't want to cast you in a bad light, but . . . I can see the water down there is shallow, and I know they drop it in winter."

More silence, more birdsong. Then Lee spoke. He spoke softer than the bird.

"O thou of little faith. Matthew 14:31."

Steve nodded.

"Faith, right. That's what all this is about. Faith trumps fact. I get it. But still, there *are* facts, and I bet they're sitting under the water. I bet they're made of wood and anchored down somehow, and every now and then they get moved somewhere else. Shall we walk down there and see?"

Lee picked up the ax and looked over our heads, maybe at a passing car, except I didn't hear a car. The bird above us had stopped singing. It was very quiet.

Lee's voice came in a whisper, then gradually got louder, until he was almost shouting.

"Blessed are they that do his commandments, that they may have right to the tree of life, and may enter in through the gates into the city. For without are dogs, and sorcerers, and whoremongers, and murderers, and idolaters, and whosoever loveth and maketh a lie."

His voice sunk to a whisper again.

"Revelation 22:14."

Lee turned and walked off into the trees. The last we saw of him was the rebel flag tattooed on his back. It rippled away through the branches and was gone.

"I'm done," Steve said. "I'm ready to go home. But first, I want a drink. Let's get drunk tonight."

As I write this, I see more and more clearly what Steve was up to, or thought he was up to. I also sense, or think I sense, the movement of God's hand.

That line Steve spun about faith trumping fact—he said something similar on the plane to Atlanta, and I bet that's what he told the people at the BBC. I can just imagine Steve pitching his film to a bunch of trendy, postmodern TV producers, all sipping mineral water through their designer beards. I'm sure he told them that he'd keep it nice and balanced, that it would contain respectful interviews with pious locals, to show how Lee Buckner changed the lives of the simple people around him. Did it even matter, in the end, if he was a fake? That was the gist of the finished film, how Steve wasn't out to expose anyone—which he obviously was—but rather to show how one man affected his small community through the power of their belief in him.

"What is truth?" Steve says to the camera. "It's what people believe. It's what *you* believe."

And so the viewers had to make up their own minds about the "miracle on the lake," aided by some heavy hints from Steve, who explains at length why he never got the miracle on film—but, of course, doesn't mention that he outright accused Lee of faking it, and that this was on film.

My brother is an idiot, as I said at the beginning. He's a clever idiot, I'll give him that, but his cleverness only heightens his idiocy, in my opinion. I'm not nearly as clever, thank God. So let's talk plainly. Steve *missed the point*. He had the whole thing upside down. Whether or not a man walked on water doesn't matter in the end, I agree. The world is full of more pressing issues. But it does matter if the man *lies* about it. It especially matters if that lie is the foundation of other people's belief in him, of my belief in him.

When we got back to the motel, the parking lot was empty. So was the office, and the door was locked. The other three went straight to the bar. I said I'd join them soon, but I didn't really want to. I wasn't in the mood to drink, which was a first for me, though it seems long ago now. These days I hardly ever drink. It's not that I disapprove of it, and I don't look down on people for drinking. I just don't do it myself. I don't need the distraction. There are other things in my life, things that interest me and make me feel good, better than any drink. That evening it was Summer. All I wanted to do was find Summer.

I sat on my bed and looked at the picture of the lion and the lamb. Every few minutes I'd open the curtain and check the parking lot. Now the light was fading, the trees losing color. Should I go to her house? I knew where she lived, and I had a car—but Steve had the key.

As I approached the bar, a truck pulled into the parking lot, its headlights sweeping the row of cars. I saw a white flash at the end of the row, and I went over to look. It was the long white Ford. Just then, a woman walked out of the bar. Summer's friend, Kendra. She saw me and waved.

"You better get in there," she said. "Summer needs looking after. She is *drunk*."

"Already?"

"Your brother's been buying shots, and Summer can't handle liquor. Your brother can't neither. He's getting kinda frisky."

They were sitting around a table near the door, with Tino and Dave facing me. Tino was in the middle of a story, I could tell. He had his arms up, palms flat in surrender, and his little egglike head was quivering with amusement. Steve's arm, I noticed, was draped over the back of Summer's chair. When Tino greeted me, the arm withdrew.

Summer grabbed my hand. "Hey, John! Where you been?"

"Where *you* been?" I said.

Tino left his story hanging and went to the bathroom, and Steve walked over to the bar. He called back to Dave, something about whiskey, and Dave got up too.

"Let's go," I said to Summer.

"But I have to say goodbye!"

"I'll tell them for you," I said. "Don't worry about it. Let's go. Now."

Outside it was almost dark. Summer fell against me, and I steered her towards her car. The doors weren't locked and I got her in the passenger seat, but then she couldn't find her key. She searched in her bag. She searched again. She started dumping things out, and that's when I saw the key. It was in the ignition.

As we drove off, Summer said she'd spent the entire day with Diane Shelby, who was on her ass and was a bitch. Finally Diane left and Summer took off early, but I wasn't in my room, so she called Kendra, since she hated going to bars alone and didn't know if I'd be there. And now she was buzzed. No, she was more than buzzed. She needed to sober up. There was water somewhere in the car. She bought it yesterday and . . .

"Here it is!"

I don't remember saying much, apart from asking Summer the way. Driving those mountain roads at night was a new experience. There were no streetlights and very few houses, and each curve seemed to jump out of the darkness. It was exactly like a film jumping, a scary film full of tree trunks and big drops.

When we reached Summer's place, I turned off the road and stopped. The driveway had a slight bump in it, and from here we couldn't see the house. I switched off the engine and hit the lights, and now I couldn't see anything at all. It took a second for my eyes to adjust. Then I saw that the sky was full of stars.

"I missed you all weekend," Summer said.

I turned and found her in the darkness, and we kissed, and kept kissing, and soon I was overtaken by the passion of my life.

I won't be more specific, because Summer wouldn't like it. Besides, you don't need specifics. We all know what people do, and saying it doesn't say much. The most I can tell you is that the moment came in waves, great waves that pushed me out of myself, beyond the reach of words, and then the waves broke over me and rolled away, and the two of us floated back to the long white car and the starry sky.

We talked a little. Summer said she didn't want me to leave, and I said I wasn't leaving yet. I'd have to pick her up in the morning and take her to work, wouldn't I? Yes, I would, and she'd make me breakfast. Seven o'clock? Seven it is, and I started the car. I drove over the bump in the driveway and we saw the lights of the house, and then we kissed and said goodbye.

I drove back to the motel and went straight to bed. The others were still drinking, I think. I remember hearing their voices later, or maybe I dreamed that, because I dreamed a lot that night. The last part of the dream has stayed with me all these years. Steve and I were at our grandparents' flat. I was young and Steve was just a toddler, barely walking. Our grandparents lived high up in a tower block, and Steve was always fascinated by the lift. In the dream, Steve sneaks out of the flat and I chase him into the lift. We ride down together, watching the green dot light up at each floor, and then the doors open and I forget about Steve, because there is Summer in her car.

"Well, can you?"

"I suppose I can," I say.

And I take the wheel, and I drive us through a sunlit meadow. Summer's laughing and eating an apple, and I'm so happy to be here. Green apple, green grass, green eyes. And then the mountains loom ahead, and I follow the road up into the trees. Up, up, up. We can smell the air, and now we can see. We're out of the trees, on top of the world. Everything is soft and blue. Mountains meet sky in soft blue waves, one after another after another. We ride those waves in our long white boat, heading ever further from shore, until the waves crash over us and—

I woke up.

It was dark outside. I didn't know what time it was, and I didn't check my watch. I was still half in that dream. But I got up and felt for my clothes and pulled them on. I stood by the door in the darkness, wondering what to do next. Then I opened the door.

I walked across the parking lot and set off up the road. I wasn't going anywhere. I was just walking. I was just a man shaking off a dream in the early morning, and as I went along, the sun came up. Soon I noticed puffs of whiteness behind the trees, and I realized where I was. One more bend in the road and I'd be at Lee Buckner's house.

The lake was covered in dazzling plumes of mist. I stopped by the big sign and looked down.

And I saw someone.

A man was standing at the top of the ramp by the house. He was only a black shape against brilliant white, but the shape was quite clear, and I knew that shape. Now the man started walking down the ramp.

I took the camera out of my pocket, set it on video and pressed record.

I am a slow person. I might talk fast, in my English way, but I do other things slowly. I learn slowly, I think, and I certainly write slowly. I started writing this in spring and it's now August. The afternoons are smothering hot, as they say around here. I like to write early, in the cool of the day. I make coffee and walk across the yard to my workshop, and then I open the laptop, reread a paragraph or two, and tap tap tap.

But this is the last morning. I'm almost done.

Sitting beside the laptop is the camera that Steve gave me ten years ago. It contains the photo of Goose and the video I shot. The video only runs for a minute, but it's perfectly in focus. I used to watch it over and over, until I could close my eyes and see each second. I still can, but I'm going to watch it again today. When I've finished writing, I'll watch it once more, and then I'll delete it.

I have never shown the video to anyone. Steve didn't ask for his camera, and I didn't offer it. After I shot the video I put the camera in my pocket, walked back to the motel and went about my day, which was a long one and ended in a different time zone, at the top of my parents' house, crashed out on my old bed.

I haven't seen much of Steve since then. The BBC aired his film, and they let him make a longer one, about American soldiers under fire in Afghanistan. Then CNN picked him up and he became the Parachute Reporter. I'd see him on TV, dropping into the middle of battles out in some desert, a bit slimmer and without the bouncy shoes, but the same old Steve. Recently my mother told me he's given up the parachuting, which may be a sign of age, or perhaps he had a bad feeling about ISIS in Iraq. Anyhow, that's history. Or it will be one day, when Hollywood makes the biopic.

Me, I went back to North Carolina a month later. I stayed with Summer, though I slept in a different room, and I didn't leave till my visa ran out. Then I returned in the spring and we married. We had the wedding in a field behind the house, beneath a dogwood tree full of white blossoms. Lee Bucker married us. A year later he baptized me in Watauga Lake, just before Summer gave birth to our daughter, Annabelle.

Lee and I became friends. He's taught me a lot about building work and helped me get jobs. In the South, where most houses are made of wood, a carpenter *is* a builder. My proudest achievement is our church. Three years ago, soon after my father died, Lee's congregation grew too big for the barn and he decided to tear it down. I argued with him, of course, but Lee said he'd keep the best wood and use it for the new floor, and I said no, *I'd* do the floor. We ended up doing it all together, apart from the pulpit, which I made here in the workshop. I found some old planks of chestnut and black walnut, and spent many hours working with the tools that Summer's father left me. I say "left me" because that's what Madge once said, shortly after the wedding. She was giving me her approval, and ever since we've got along well, mostly. Madge can be kind of abrupt, but I'm abrupt myself, according to Summer. She doesn't say "abrupt," though. She says "nervous."

My own mother has visited twice, and we've taken Deedee and Annabelle to England several times. The last time was my father's funeral, which was also the last time I saw Steve, and met his girlfriend. She is a news anchor in LA and talks with huge excitement, as if she's always giving you a news flash. Summer found her puzzling, but she likes my mother. Summer really likes my mother. Sometimes she talks about moving to England, since my mother won't move over here. Lee talks about it too. He has been encouraging me to establish my own church somewhere else. Maybe that's why I've taken to writing, as a way of sifting my memories, of remembering where I've been and deciding where to go. But I don't think I'm going anywhere, at least not to England. My duties are to my wife and two children and our church. Now and then I stand in for Lee at Sunday service, but I am not an inspiring pastor. Being inspirational is what Lee does—and what Steve does, come to think of it. They're both great at firing people up, but not so interested in follow-through, in life's little details. I'm more like my father. I mind the details. I notice all the things that no one wants to hear about, like moss on the roof and wild onions spreading in the front yard. That's my line of work.

Now, I know what you're probably thinking, because I've often wondered about it: why didn't I show the video to Steve? Lee wouldn't have been pleased, but that's not the answer, and neither is the fact that Steve would have been just too pleased. Before I started writing, I didn't have an answer. I still don't have an easy one, but I'll do my best to explain myself.

Life is miraculous. You are a miracle, and I am a miracle, and so is the space between us, which in this case is the page that I am writing and you are reading. Isn't that a miracle? I believe it is, and that miracles are all around us. If the word "miracle" bothers you, replace it with "beauty." Beauty is all around us. We don't see it much of the time, because we're too busy hiding from it, or looking for it elsewhere, but it's right in front of our noses. And occasionally we do see it. Something happens and our eyes open. Suddenly we wake up. When the plane touched down in Atlanta and that little kid started screaming, and the tough guy turned around—to me, that was a miracle. I thought he'd say something to the mother, or even the child, but he didn't say a word, and yet the child stopped screaming. When something like that happens, we're astonished. Then, in time, we forget. I said I'd never forget that moment, but I will. Having written about it, I can feel it starting to fade. Why? Why do we forget?

Because we change. Each miracle changes us, and as it does, it loses its importance. The miracle itself ceases to matter. In a sense, it stops being a miracle. It becomes part of who we are, what we see. Miracles are everywhere and miracles are nowhere, like the hand of God.

I didn't show the video to Steve because it wasn't meant for Steve. It was meant for me. And now I have to let it go. I have to close this laptop and turn on the camera and watch the screen.

About the Author

JACOB BEAVER was born in Kenya in 1964. He grew up in England and lived in London for twenty years, working in publishing and as an editor at the Royal College of Art. In 2007 he married in East Tennessee, where he now lives. His writing has appeared in the *London Review of Books* and British magazines. Find him online at jacobbeaver.com.